"Get ou… you silly peeping Tom!

Garrett had let go of Kate and was swearing, inexplicably shaking his fist toward the wall. In the darkness of the bedroom, a patch of blue, like the haze of cigarette smoke, hung near the ceiling.

"What's wrong?" Kate asked, clutching the top sheet to cover her bare breasts. "Is it—"

"Mac," Garrett growled. "Having an out-of-body trip. My colleague specializes in that kind of experiment."

"You mean he can drop in on us like that anytime? Talk about taking your research home…."

"Now, Kate, I don't think he'd do that now that he knows what we're up to," Garrett teased. The blue glow against the wall faded into black.

"Are you kidding?" she said in a huff. "He …bably went for popcorn and a beer, the …er to enjoy the show!" She leaned over the …, grabbing her clothes. "I'm leaving, …rrett. I've had all I can take when it comes … *sensory* experiences."

As she started wrestling her clothes on, Garrett pulled her to him. "I'll be the judge of that," he murmured….

Kara Galloway has now joined the world of romance with her first Temptation title, *Sleight Of Heart*. A well-established mystery writer for the past twenty years, Kara used to think that it was "just easier to think of reasons for people to kill each other than fall in love." Happily for us, she had a change of heart. Kara says she especially enjoyed writing *Sleight Of Heart* because of the humor in the story and the fascinating research she did on magic and the paranormal.

Kara lives in Colorado with her husband. Her two sons are grown and flown.

Sleight of Heart

KARA GALLOWAY

Harlequin Books

TORONTO • NEW YORK • LONDON
AMSTERDAM • PARIS • SYDNEY • HAMBURG
STOCKHOLM • ATHENS • TOKYO • MILAN

To my parents, who have to share the blame

Published November 1990

ISBN 0-373-25422-9

SLEIGHT OF HEART

Printed in U.S.A.

1

Kathy the Great, aka Kate Christopher, slumped gracelessly over the kitchen table, blue eyes at half-mast, waiting for the phone to ring. The overhead fluorescent turned her white terry robe tattletale gray, her tanned skin muddy, her tangled blond hair seaweed green. In the final throes of a spring cold, she felt as bad as she looked.

Across the white-walled, walnut-cupboarded room, Aunt Corliss rocked and kept her company. Every snowy curl in place, size forty print dress as crisp as if the day were just beginning, Corliss smiled vaguely at the long-barreled black pistol she was polishing. The clock in the hall gonged three times.

"Where did you say Mr. Bing is performing tonight?" the elderly lady asked, coasting the rocker to a stop and aiming the gun at the ceiling.

Sniffing, Kate traced the oilcloth's pattern with a pink fingernail. "The art museum. A fund-raiser for the Denver Zoo."

Corliss pulled the trigger and a white scarf that read Bang unfurled. She spread it on her lap, inspecting it for places to mend.

The phone jolted them both. Kate put her hand on it and waited for the third ring. "Hello?"

There was a moment's hesitation on the other end of the line as if the man who'd called didn't recognize her husky voice. "Hello! May I speak to Katherine, Kathy the Great, Queen of Magic?"

"This is she," she croaked modestly.

"Kathy, my dear. I'm sorry to bother you when you're under the weather." Then she heard him say through his palm on the mouthpiece, "Of course, she's under the weather. Have you ever heard of anyone being over the weather?" and then muffled laughter.

"What can I do for you, Captain Bing?" she asked.

"We're having a little gala here at the art museum tonight. Would you mind helping us out with a demonstration of telepathic power?"

"I'd be happy to help. What would you like me to do?"

"A member of our fine audience has kindly volunteered to select a card out of a full deck. He'll form a mental image of it and try to send that image to you telepathically. We're amplifying your voice and everyone can hear you, so now don't tell me to go to hell."

She waited for the laughter on the other end of the line to ebb. "I will do my best to see the card your volunteer has selected." The haughty enunciation was spoiled by a muffled cough at the end.

Then she heard unintelligible murmurings, and she pictured Jamie Bing in his ebony tuxedo and blindingly white shirt, fanning out the cards to a self-conscious volunteer who hadn't been on a stage since he got his high school diploma.

Bing's voice deepened and loudened into words directed at his volunteer. "This one here?" he asked. "All right, hold on to it. Now just concentrate on the card. Think."

"Kathy?" he bellowed into her ear.

"Yes?"

"We're ready."

"All right." She examined her fingernails. Ace, deuce, or trey. After enough suspense-building silence, she began. "Blood. I see blood."

"Kathy. Kathy? Don't get carried away here. We don't want to solve a murder. We just want to identify a playing card." A ripple of crowd reaction ensued.

"Then it must be a heart. A blood-red heart."

Aunt Corliss snorted and shook her head.

Bing's cue—"Is that right, Mary?" zinged along the line. *Trey*.

"Captain Bing?" she called, suddenly envisioning her crisp, pink bed with its soft, cool pillow. Final curtain time. "It's as if it's— I sense a low number. Not a two, but close to a two. One, two—" Long pause. "Three," she announced. "It's a three of hearts."

She could hear the applause.

"Thank you, Kathy. Three of hearts it is. Thank you and good night."

"Good night." She cradled the phone, sighed, and then pushed up from the table.

"I don't know how you do it," Corliss said, reaching into the snake charmer basket at her feet to dredge up thread, scissors, and thimble.

"You do, too."

"I guess you've told me. How does it go again?"

"If Bing says to his volunteer, 'This,' it's a diamond. 'This one,' it's a club. 'This one here,' it's a heart. If he doesn't say any of that, it's a spade."

"Yes. And something else he says narrows the thirteen cards of the suits into groups."

"'Think,' tells me its an ace, deuce or trey. 'Now think,' means a four, five, six. And so on up to silence for a king."

"Oh, yes. And how did you know it was the three and not ace or deuce?" Corliss sighted through the needle, thread poised to stab the eye.

"When I name the suit, Bing asks the volunteer, 'Right?' or 'That's right?' or 'Is that right?' for the first, second, or third card in the previously signaled group." Kate shuffled toward the hall.

"It's so complicated," Corliss complained. "It would be easier to really do it by ESP."

A door slammed and brisk footsteps creaked the hardwood floor. Kate's other aunt, Hank, bustled in and dumped a grocery bag on the table. "Lookie what I found," she said, rooting out bananas, grapes, and peaches with abandon.

"Bruised fruit?" Corliss hazarded a guess.

"Handles!" Aunt Hank crowed, holding up the blister pack triumphantly.

Kate took the package and bent it toward the light. "Perfect."

"I thought so. The little copper dragons eating their tails seemed kind of medieval. Isn't it wonderful what you can get at the grocery store these days?"

Kate crossed the floor to show it to Corliss, who nodded and asked, "What are you making now, Hank?"

"A bunny box."

Corliss understood this cryptic appellation at once. "Kate! You're going to add rabbits to your act?"

"I doubt it. The birthday party you booked me for next weekend? The father wants me to surprise the kid with a puppy. It won't be easy. Puppies are a lot noisier than rabbits. I may have to knock him out first."

Hank squealed a protest before realizing Kate wasn't serious.

Knotting her thread with a vicious thumb-finger twist, Corliss lifted herself out of the rocker, laid her strange sewing on the seat, and crossed over to the fruit-strewn table. She selected a banana and a peach and began absentmindedly polishing them on the front of her dress. "Did you get cheese?"

"Cheese, cheese," Hank muttered, stirring the groceries with one hand.

Kathy lounged in the doorway and fondly watched her father's sisters. They were identical twins, but because their lives had taken them in different directions, they had become psychologically and physically very different from each other. Corliss, married in her teens to a government diplomat, had lived in five countries, borne eight children, and gained fifty pounds. Hannah, only minutes younger than her sister, had adopted a masculine name for the protection it afforded a single lady living alone in the city. Hank had also learned to take care of herself by mastering plumbing, electricity, carpentry, and auto mechanics. Furthermore, it had been great for the figure.

The two of them looked like a before-and-after diet plan ad.

"Night, ladies," Kate called, turning the corner into the dark.

"Night, dear," they chorused. "Are you working tomorrow?" Corliss tacked on.

"Yup." Saturday was a busy day in the singing telegrams biz. She hoped her throat would cooperate.

"Here's the cheese," Hank rejoiced.

"Mmm-hmm. Where's the tortilla chips?"

"Tortilla chips, tortilla chips . . ."

Kate felt her way upstairs to bed.

IN THE MORNING, cooking smells roused her. Not bacon or hot chocolate or any traditional morning aroma. This was tangy tomato, onion, and garlic.

Kate's aunts were coauthoring a cookbook. Every meal for the past four months had been a culinary experiment, some decidedly less successful than others. Kate knuckled sleep from her eyes and girded herself in the terry cloth robe to confront breakfast.

Hank had slept on her hair wrong. One wayward lock stuck straight out on the side like a rearview mirror. She stirred a pot which appeared to contain molten lava. Hunched at the table, writing furiously in a spiral notebook, Corliss enlightened Kate, "Sauce for Italian omelet. Ready in five minutes. Call Bing."

Glancing at her watch, Kate reached for the phone. "What's he want this early?"

Hank held up the spoon and frowned at the red tar clinging to it. "You sound better, Kate. Corliss, is this thick enough?"

Kate dialed Bing's number and waited patiently while it rang.

"Bing," he growled after seven rings, as if having to answer the phone was imposing on his precious time.

"Hi. Your humble servant here."

"Ahh, Kathy. You have your voice back. I have a job for you."

Behind her, Corliss exclaimed, "Tomato candy! Let it go to the hard ball stage."

"What kind of job?" asked Kathy.

"The role of your career. Calling for all your skill, intelligence, daring, deviousness."

"Sounds good." Kate slithered into a chair, the phone in her lap, and her heels hooked on the the center rung. "Tell me more." Hank set a cup of scalding coffee at her elbow and Kate nodded her thanks.

"In person. Over lunch, perhaps?"

This was not an invitation to dine at his expense. Jamie Bing lived in a deluxe condominium with a view of the Rockies. He wore custom-tailored suits and drove a Porsche. He had not accumulated a fortune by giving anything away, including meals.

"I'll check in with Up and Away to see what my schedule is today. Then I'll call you back. Are you at home?"

"The shop." When he wasn't performing magic, Bing sold it, from what looked like a walk-in closet fronting on Denver's refurbished Sixteenth Street.

Kate signed off and dialed her second employer, the Up and Away Singing Greeting and Balloons People, Inc. She sampled the coffee and cringed.

"It's a dandy day at Up and Away," Doretta on switchboard singsonged.

"Hey, Retta."

"Hey, magic lady. How's tricks?" Doretta's usual greeting never failed to make Doretta laugh.

Interrupting the giggling, Kate asked, "How many deliveries have you got for me today?"

"Well, I wasn't sure you'd feel up to any. So none. But wait a momento." Kate could hear papers rustling. "You look better in a tutu than Selma does, so you can have that one. Then there's a balloon bouquet scheduled to go to a bar in Colfax that Selma's chicken to do, and another one scheduled for ten tonight, but Selma wants to get off work before ten."

Selma was the owner's shy, underweight, overindulged daughter. Surprisingly, Kate not only liked her but did some of the overindulging herself.

"What times on the others?" She made a grasping motion at Corliss, who tore a sheet from her notebook to pass over along with the pen. Kate jotted down numbers, mmhmming. "Nothing before two o'clock then? See you at about one."

AT ELEVEN-FORTY, Kate sat across a café booth from Jamie Bing, waiting for the pancakes she'd ordered, tomato candy for breakfast having left much to be desired.

Without his stage makeup on, Bing was an unimposing man—an undramatic accountant or Realtor, perhaps. His narrow shoulders, slightly receding chin, more than slightly receding hairline, and stained smoker's teeth might have explained why he had never found a mate. Or maybe he just wouldn't pop for the license.

He touched the back of his head, the knot of his tie, the handle of his fork, and then winked conspiratorially at Kate. "It's something you've never done before," he announced just above a whisper.

Wondering how he could be so sure, she merely raised her eyebrows.

"It will pay well," he continued, barely moving his lips. "Have you ever heard of CROPS?"

She leaned forward, wanting to cup a hand behind her ear. "Craps?"

There was nothing restrained about Bing's burst of laughter. "You've got that right," he finally sputtered. "But it's C-R-O-P-S."

Feeling the resentment of a sucker not in on the joke, Kate said stiffly, "Is that an acronym for something?"

"Central Rockies Organization for Paranormal Studies. They have a laboratory over in the foothills north of Golden."

"What, exactly, do they study?"

A plate was thumped under Kate's chin. The pancakes looked charbroiled. Probably foreseeing an argument, the waitress beat a hasty retreat.

Bing lifted the lid of his cheeseburger and flooded it with catsup. "They do so-called scientific experiments involving telepathy, clairvoyance, out of body travel, that kind of garbage."

When he bit into his sandwich, Kate hastily averted her eyes. She began skinning the worst off her pancakes. "So?"

"So it's not right for people to waste money on lame-brained stuff like that. It's not right to mislead the gullible public into believing wild, occult claims." His voice had risen with his indignation. He glanced around the almost empty restaurant and leaned forward to whisper, "It's up to us magicians to expose those charlatans."

Still not sure why he was so het up, Kate put too much syrup on her plate and began to eat.

"This is what we do." Bing's hand and mouth reminded Kate of Dracula. She pointedly handed him her napkin. "They always need volunteers for their experiments. You go up there, incognito, and sign on for testing, and once they're convinced you're a psychic whiz kid, we'll tell the media how you did it all by magic, sleight of hand, sleight of brain, trickery. CROPS will be a laughingstock and you'll be famous."

She wrinkled her nose. "I don't want to be famous. Why don't you do it yourself?"

"Because the head warlock up there, Garrett Brody, knows me. We've debated each other both in print and in person." He twisted his head as if his collar hurt. "And I always win, but he never admits it."

How could Bing's cheeseburger be gone when he'd been doing all the talking? Magic, Kate guessed. She shoveled another gooey bite into her mouth.

"I'm taking the act to Las Vegas for a couple of weeks. You'll have some free time while I'm away," Bing wheedled. "Why don't you give this a whirl?"

Stalling, Kate asked, "Minda going with you?"

Of course she was. Minda, Bing's other protégée, was always his assistant on the road, even though it usually meant cutting her university classes. So far, she'd spent four years as a freshman. She was aiming at a career in medicine—gynecology.

Despite Kate's efforts to distract him Bing wasn't sidetracked. "I'll draw you a map of how to find the CROPS lab."

"Aww, Bing, I don't want to—"

"I'll pay you one thousand dollars."

"One thousand?" She was amazed he could say it without stuttering. The back of her neck tingled, but it was mostly because of a solemn toddler hanging over the booth behind her, breathing on it.

"Plus travel expenses."

"Bing—"

"Plus whatever the lab pays its volunteers."

"Bing! Are you crazy? You're offering a fortune for what? What does my diddling some misguided scientist's research do for you?"

"All right, I confess." He gave the room another nervous survey and waited tight-lipped for the toddler and family to shuffle past as they left the café. "I want to write a book. An exposé. A refutation of the proparanormal titles that are being published right and left. I want to go down in history as the man who restored reason to a society in danger of foundering on occult hogwash."

She hoped he could write better than he could lecture. It took her two tries to lay down her syrupy fork. "There's no such thing as ESP."

"Agreed."

"Those guys at CROPS shouldn't be wasting their minds and time and energy on nonsense."

"Agreed again."

"A thousand dollars?"

"Half in advance." He nodded, reeling her in.

Kate sighed and pushed plates aside. "Draw me the damn map."

2

AT TWO O'CLOCK, Kate punched a doorbell with one point of her wand and brushed down the skirt of her pink sequined tutu, polite smile at the ready. The elderly gentleman who let her in clasped his hands over his heart in admiration. He led her into a furniture-glutted bedroom smelling of deep heating rub. A second elderly gentleman lay in the bed. He scowled at the ceiling while she sang the basic birthday jingle and tied balloons to the bedpost. The first man thanked her, pressed a quarter tip into her palm and propositioned her to "pas de deux" him on his next birthday. Then she went on to make her next delivery.

Selma had been right to avoid the Colfax bar. When she paused outside the place to slide the penlight Mace into her palm, Kate graded the dive with a capital *D* for dirty, drugged, and dangerous. Though she'd prudently changed from her tutu into an all-enveloping rabbit suit, she felt every eye skinning her as she shoved the balloons at the bartender and made her escape.

With a couple of hours to kill before her last delivery, Kate went home for supper. Parking at the crumbling curb, she paused to enjoy the twilight which softened and flattered the aging neighborhood like a Vaseline-smeared camera lens.

The Christopher place had been the Christopher place since it was first built in 1903. A saltbox with a generous porch on the front and a fringe of untidy shrubbery, it had never been *Better Homes and Gardens* material. But Kate allowed a foolish attack of sentimentality to dampen her eyes before shaking herself free of it and tramping inside to discover what unspeakable leftovers the refrigerator might hold.

Hank sat at the red-checked oilcloth covered table, her face buried in her hands.

Kate's heart gave a little hiccup of apprehension. "Hank?" she asked softly.

The narrow, knotty-veined fingers spread apart, and Hank peered between them. "Hello, dear," she said in her usual, sweetly casual way.

"Uh, you all right?"

"Oh, yes." Her voice was muffled by her palms. "It's only a test."

Relaxing, Kate strolled to the white, gently vibrating refrigerator. "What kind of test?"

"ESP."

Kate jerked the door open much wider than she'd intended. "ESP?" She took out an onion and stared at it uncomprehendingly.

"Corliss was reading in a magazine that twins are especially sensitive to reading each other's minds. She's gone upstairs to concentrate on some object, and I'm supposed to guess what it is."

"I see. Sorry to have bothered you then." Kate returned the onion and took out a carton of milk.

Without turning around, Hank said, "That one's gone sour. Try the other."

Kate tipped back her head and studied the intricate curlicues and geometric shapes of the white tin ceiling. Then she quietly exchanged the milks and began to assemble a turkey club sandwich, deliberately switching her thoughts to such trivial matters as what she should wear Monday to infiltrate CROPS.

Corliss came clumping downstairs a few minutes later.

"Mama's handmirror," Hank said.

"Right," Corliss said.

"Coincidence," Kate said and, seeing her aunts' expressions, quickly added, "but very skillfully done!"

THE 10 P.M.DELIVERY was to a good address in the foothills, so the harem outfit seemed safe. Dressed in costume jewelry and gauze pantaloons, and carrying two dozen rainbow-colored balloons in each hand, Kate lightly kicked the apartment door. Laughter leaked into the hall as the door opened and a young woman with a Little Orphan Annie hairdo motioned Kate inside. Because the vestibule was too narrow for the balloons, they were handed from party goer to party goer.

"You're going to sing a birthday message?" the woman in the "Annie" hairdo confirmed brusquely.

"That's what was ordered."

"You don't mind waiting in the closet," the woman said as she unlatched a door at Kate's elbow. Things began to ooze out onto their feet—a tennis racket, a baseball glove, a running shoe. "Annie" fought the spill back inside and slammed the door.

"The bedroom then," she said, winding a path through the living room. At the far wall, she inched aside a sliding door, listened for landslides, then pushed Kate through the gap into the bedroom.

"It's a surprise party and he isn't here yet," "Annie" said, shuddering the door shut.

It was dark inside. Kate imagined she heard an echo to her breathing. Hastily she patted the wall for a light switch, failed to find one, and quietly slid the door open an eye's width. In view was the hall and, on both her right and left peripheries, a room full of milling strangers.

"Annie" was shushing them, shutting off lamps. "Sit down somewhere, everyone. He'll be here any minute."

Kate mentally rehearsed the dippy song. Happy, happy birthday— Oh, no. What's his name? Jerry? Gary. Happy, happy birthday, Gary—

"Ssst," "Annie" warned loudly.

Kate put her eye closer to the crack of light. Into the hush, a key scraped a lock. More silence. The front door exploded against the wall, jerking Kate so that she lost her focus.

A single male voice shouted, "Surprise!" Silence. No one seconded the exhortation.

Kate squinted at the silhouette of a tall, lean man standing at the threshold of the apartment, his hair haloed by an outside wall lamp. He repeated, "Surprise!" and switched on the living-room chandelier.

Groans. Odd acoustics made some of them seem to come from behind Kate.

"Annie" shrieked, "How'd you know? Gary, you rat!" She moved and her back blocked Kate's view. "Okay, which one of you let the cat out of the bag?"

A masculine arm crept around "Annie's" shoulders and squeezed, showing off tanned muscles. "Nobody told me. You should know better than to try to surprise me, Ann."

Temporarily distracted by the discovery that she'd actually guessed the hostess's name, Kate missed their next exchange.

"What's to eat?" Gary said, as he was walking Ann toward the center of the room.

"You mean you don't know?" Ann drawled sarcastically.

Gary reached into the guests, shaking hands, patting backs, trading insults.

"Wait!" Ann commanded. "By God, I'll surprise you yet." She swiveled toward the bedroom.

Kate straightened up and adjusted the straps on her skimpy halter. Behind her in the dark, someone or some *thing* gave a long, hissing sigh that ended with the unmistakable sound of teeth clicking.

Before Ann had even touched the door, Kate pushed it open and leaped through. In spite of her fright, her aim was good. She bumped to a stop against Gary and teetered on her toes in his spontaneous embrace.

Lifting her nose from his musky-clean shirt front, she looked past his square jaw and straight nose into a pair of startled gray eyes. He grinned slowly, like the Big Bad Wolf.

"You win, Ann. I'm surprised," he said, licking his chops.

Kate twitched her chin over her shoulder. "There's someone in there."

He didn't slacken his hold although she'd regained her equilibrium. "Probably my wimpy dog and my wimpy philodendrons."

"Dog?" Kate repeated ingenuously.

Keeping a firm hold on her and turning her around, he put thumb and finger to his mouth and whistled. "Smedley. Here, boy."

A shorthaired white dog stepped from the shadows, doing a Bogart imitation with his teeth. He seemed torn between welcoming his master and hiding from everyone else. His stubby tail finally wagged him out of sight behind the bed.

Ann shooed her fingers at Kate. "Go ahead."

Extracting herself from Gary's pleasantly forceful grasp and turning to face him, Kate retreated three steps, ostentatiously cleared her throat and began. "Happy, happy birthday, Gary, from your many, many friends, who all wish you joy and gladness and good luck that never ends. . . ."

All ten, deadly dull verses.

Usually the recipients of this protracted melodramatic attention squirmed, looked away, and turned red. But not Gary. Arms folded, standing patiently still and straight, he watched her with a lopsided, all-knowing smile.

It was old pro Kate who fidgeted, avoided eye contact, and blushed.

WITH THE MONDAY MORNING SUN at her back and Bing's map taped to the dashboard of her perky red Honda, Kate wound along secondary roads toward Golden. Her cold seemed well and truly over, KBCO was playing a block of Peter Gabriel records, and the breeze that streamed through the sunroof smelled green. She tapped her fingers on the steering wheel and grinned, remembering Saturday night.

Gary had insisted she stay for a celebratory glass of champagne. Left up to him, she could have stayed for the whole party. But it was against Up and Away's rules, and although it didn't bother Kate, Ann—his sister—obviously disapproved of fraternizing with the hired help. Kate swallowed her drink faster than was comfortable and took her leave.

The dumb part was that because she didn't know Gary's last name, she couldn't benefit from this enlightened era of female initiative-taking by calling him. She knew his address, however, so she could send a note—addressed to "occupant," maybe!

A red light allowed her to study the map for a minute. She craned her neck looking for a highway number on the intersection, decided she was on course, and spurred the Honda into Golden.

It was Gary's quirky smile that had gotten to her first, and then his gray eyes gleaming with intelligence and amusement. Kate always liked that in a man—a sense of humor. She didn't want a clown or a practical joker, but she'd love to have someone easygoing to laugh with at the end of a boring or frustrating day.

A bristle-faced man driving a pickup truck—and possessing *no* visible sense of humor—zigzagged around her when she slowed to check street signs.

Gary's lean, hard body, Kate had to admit, had claimed her attention, too. And his shock of dark hair just begged to be finger-combed. Face it. The man was probably spoken for, unavailable, attached, because he was definitely too good to be true.

Tasteful silver script on a black sign announced that the Central Rockies Organization for Paranormal Studies was five miles to her left. She made the turn and followed the steadily rising road into khaki-colored vegetation and rusty boulders.

A tickle of stage fright intruded as she let her images of Gary go and began to imagine Dr. Brody. He'd be a stooped, rat-faced man in a white coat, hugging a clipboard to his chest. Showing her a falsely social smile from the nose down, he'd bow her into a chrome and white testing room with one-way mirrors and hard plastic chairs six inches too low for the long, empty tables in the room.

Was she psychic? A piece of cake.

She overshot the entrance with its unassuming black sign and narrow dirt driveway. Hanging a U-turn on the quiet highway, Kate reminded herself not to mention her main, *magic,* occupation. If Doc Brody could believe in folks bending spoons with their minds, he'd believe that she made a decent living singing telegrams.

The car jiggled and danced up the rutted lane for half a mile before a building came into view. Kate blinked and braked. Not the low, clinical white stucco and glass she'd been expecting, this was a three-story Victorian house girdled with porches, painted a pale lemon-yellow with charcoal-gray gingerbread trim. On either side of the black double doors, a clay urn fountained white petunias.

The driveway took a gentle sweep to the right and ended in a grassy apron for parking behind the house. One four-wheel drive and one station wagon, both covered in red dust, were already parked there.

Kate jerked up the emergency brake and nervously wiped her palms on her denim skirt. She knew she'd be fine once she was inside and "on." It was hanging around in the wings that was nerve-racking. Accordingly, she climbed out of the car, hooked the strap of her shoulder bag into place, and strode confidently toward the back porch, which was a smaller version of the front, right down to the petunias.

The shallow steps and gray porch floor were eroded toward the center from decades of traffic. Searching for a doorbell and not finding it, Kate paused, debating whether to knock or just walk in. She decided to do both.

"Anyone home?" she called lightly, rapping on the doorjamb as she stepped over the threshold.

The hall ran straight from backdoor to front entrance. Except for a dotted line of carpet runners that had once been patterned in flowers, the hall was empty. There was a row of closed doors on either side, and, between the doors, faded paintings of mountains, romanticized gardens, and seascapes.

Kate found herself tiptoeing toward the other end, looking for an open room, a receptionist. Some of the doors sported brass nameplates—Records, Supplies, Testing, Rest room. Almost to the opposite end, she discovered twin staircases pirouetting on either side of the hall to regroup as a balcony on the second floor overlooking the tiny foyer.

Tilting her head back, she timidly inquired, "Hello?" After a period of unbroken silence she tried it again, louder.

Somewhere a chair squeaked. Shoes scuffed bare floor. Kate smoothed back her hair and waited.

"Could I help you?"

He was just as she'd pictured him. The pointy-chinned face peering over the balcony railing at her was showing teeth in a parody of a smile. His white lab coat hung open over an Hawaiian shirt and Bermuda shorts. When he leaned closer, his clipboard clacked against the wooden railing.

"Uhh, I'm here to volunteer? For paranormal testing?" Kate felt an overwhelming desire to be home practicing her puppy-out-of-the-box trick.

"Had you filled out an application?" He shaded his eyes with one hand, as if she were too bright in the dim hall.

"No. I just came. Maybe you don't need volunteers right now?" she said, trying not to sound too hopeful.

A thousand dollars would be nice. On the other hand, nobody would hear screaming in this godforsaken place.

"We always need fresh blood," he laughed. Maybe he *could* read minds. "Come on up."

Hugging a newel post, she listened to the quiet building. "Am I too early?"

"No, no. We don't have normal hours. We have paranormal hours," he said with the ease of frequent use.

Wondering if she would ever pass this way again, Kate marched up the steps.

He struck off down a hall that was a carbon copy of the one below. "How did you know about us?" From the back, with the knee-length lab coat flapping over hairy, bare legs, he looked like a flasher.

"Umm, a friend of mine had heard about CROPS somewhere and said I should look you up—since I seem to have some ability in that direction."

He made a smart turn in through a door labeled Office. "Ever done any psy-tests before?" He put the clipboard on the peak of a mountain of papers covering one of the two desks in the room and began to collect forms from various drawers.

"No, I never have."

She strolled forward to admire the floor-to-ceiling view. Except for the dirt streaks on the window, it could have been a painting—the muted browns and greens of a meadow outlined by red boulders. A beaver creek meandered through the center, and a gray peak on the horizon had snagged one cotton-ball cloud in an otherwise all-blue sky.

"Why don't you just sit here and fill these out?" He indicated the other, less cluttered desk.

The old-fashioned oak swivel chair was as noisy as it looked decrepit. All the woodwork in the room needed a strong dose of furniture wax. Kate accepted the papers and ballpoint pen and bent over the first question. *Name?*

Kathy the Great wasn't famous enough to make a lie necessary. She confidently printed, "Christopher, Kate Allison," and skidded the "n" toward the top of the page as his voice crackled over her shoulder.

"Kate, is it? Would you like some coffee?"

"Thank you, that would be nice. Black," she answered, writing her real age—thirty-three; she intended to lie as little as possible.

He swished out of the room. *Address, phone number. Occupation?* She abbreviated it to "mess delivery," hesitated, and decided that wasn't far from the truth. Her pen hovered over the block for "sex."

"Please don't put 'Y' in there. It's an old joke."

For the second time, a voice above her shoulder startled her. She marked an "F" in the box before looking around at the man seating himself at the other desk.

Plaid shirt, jeans, thick black hair, alert gray eyes, thin nose, lips bracketed by smile lines—Gary.

3

THE PEN JUMPED OUT of her fingers and rolled to the toe of his left shoe. He bent to retrieve it and, handing it across to her, recognized her.

"I know you." He pinched his mouth, thinking. "You're the singer with the balloons."

Just then the man she'd assumed was Dr. Brody came gliding in, holding a paper towel under her coffee mug. He raised his eyebrows at her.

"He makes me sound like a stripper," Kate said.

"What a coincidence," Gary marveled. "Mac, this is the little lady who was waiting to surprise me in my bedroom Saturday night."

Kate groaned and covered her eyes. Mac leaned over her shoulder to read what she'd put down for occupation.

She whispered, "I thought you were Dr. Brody."

Pretending to shudder at the thought, Mac whispered back, "Alas, I'm only Igor."

"How do you do," she said, her mind occupied elsewhere. Then, looking at Dr. Brody, she said, "And your name is Gary, right?"

"Gary stands for Garrett. Only my overbearing sister calls me that cutesy name. Everyone else calls me Gare or Garrett."

"What he likes to be called is Dr. Brody. With as much reverence as you can muster," his colleague said behind one hand at ordinary volume.

"Igor, here, is Doctor MacArthur Thayer, Colorado's leading authority on OOBs."

"OOBs?"

"Out of body experiences. Ever have one?"

Kate grimaced. "Maybe once, at a Rolling Stones concert."

"It's a wonderful feeling," Mac assured her. "Floating, flying, unhampered by gravity-weighed flesh. I like to take a spin about once a week. Go visit my mama in Canada, drop in at the White House, spy on my ex-wife and her latest playmate."

"And what's your specialty, Dr. Brody?"

"Garrett. I'm interested in everything. Currently, let's see—" He tipped back the chair and crossed his long legs on the desktop, unmindful of the avalanche it set off. "It's distinguishing colors by touch and teaching houseplants how to read."

Trying to remember when she'd stepped through the looking glass, Kate glanced at the next page of her questionnaire. The first question was: *Have you ever predicted a disaster?*

"Once," she wrote in the space. "Including now."

While Kate studied the questionnaire, Garrett studied her. Nice face with lips turning up even while her mind was on the boring paperwork. A pert nose rosy with sunburn, or maybe as a result of the cold she'd mentioned having. Shoulder-length blond hair that was either naturally curly or enjoyed a darn good hairdresser. Trim body.

She shifted abruptly, and he swerved his gaze to the closest paper lying on his desk until he thought she was safely absorbed in her writing again. Then, he continued his inventory of her.

Very trim body. Lovely line from collarbone to waist, swelling just enough and not too much. Legs so smooth and brown he had to stare at them for some time to decide they were bare and not stockinged.

Mac, who'd left the office on some errand of his own, came back and inconsiderately stood between Garrett and the view, compounding the intrusion by asking a work-related question. Sighing, Garrett forced his mind back to more mundane matters.

"SO YOU THINK YOU'VE HAD some psychic experiences?" Garrett said, leafing through her completed questionnaire.

Kate shrugged modestly. "Maybe. A friend and I were fooling around with a deck of cards, and I seemed to be able to guess which one he'd selected."

"Uh-huh. We don't test with cards or dice."

"No?"

"Too boring." He smacked the papers against his knee in a let's-get-on-with-it way. "It doesn't matter whether you think you're psychic or not."

Oh-oh. Was he on to her already, and about to throw her out?

"Everyone's born with some psychic ability. Most of us don't notice it and let it atrophy. Some of the world's most gifted psychics first tried it on a dare, so to speak, and couldn't at first believe what they were doing." He stood up. "There are a couple of things I'd like to try with you."

Surreptitiously eying his shrunk-to-fit jeans, she could think of a couple of things herself. But he was all business, flipping open an appointment book he'd dredged up from the foundation of his paper tower.

"Isn't there something I could participate in this morning, since I'm already here?" She wanted to perform her little deception and get it over with.

"There's the colors thing. Doesn't take long. Remote viewing requires some setting up, so maybe you'd come back for that another day this week?"

She shrugged. "Whatever."

"Let's run downstairs."

A clipboard materialized in his hand; he could probably pull a rabbit and some doves from that desk, too. He touched her elbow and static electricity snapped.

He'd used the word "run" advisedly. Kate's narrow skirt forced her to take mincing steps, leaving her at a respectful distance.

"So how's the singing telegram business?"

"Fine, fine. And how long has CROPS been operating?"

"Almost three years. I bet you could tell some funny stories. About your experiences."

"I'm sure you could, too. Where does CROPS get its funding?"

They flew down the stairs, Garrett looking loose-kneed easy and Kate clinging to the banister.

"Trust fund of a wealthy gent interested in the occult. That slave girl costume you had on the other night was really fetching."

"Thanks. Do you have trouble getting volunteers?"

They cleared the foyer and strode into the lower hall.

"Sometimes. Do you have a steady beau?" He herded her through the door marked Testing.

"Not right this minute. Is that a one-way mirror?"

"Yes. Want to have dinner with me tonight?"

"Yes." Trying not to pant, she sank onto a plastic straight chair too low for the table beside it. "Do you always walk like that?"

Garrett looked down at himself. "Like what?"

She shook her head in amusement. "Never mind. I'm ready to be tested, but I warn you, I have a low pain threshold."

His slow grin made a tickle ripple through her stomach. "How's your threshold for pleasure?"

She pretended to be distracted by one leg of the chair being too short, shifting it around in search of a compatible floorboard. Garrett walked over to a black storage cabinet and rummaged through its shelves, humming Happy Days Are Here Again. Kate stood up, exasperated, and traded chairs. This one had *two* legs too short.

The room was as bleak as its furniture, with three khaki-colored walls and one a very off-white. The windows afforded a view of the driveway snaking below a cliff so emaciated by erosion, tree roots hung exposed like skeletal ribs.

Garrett clanged the cabinet shut, laid a stack of cardboard squares at the far end of her table, and tossed her a black scarf. "Blindfold."

"Pin the tail on the donkey?" She smoothed the material on her thigh and fanfolded it.

"Colors." He spread out the cardboard squares in front of her. Each was a different, bright, pure color, reminding Kate of crayons she had known and loved. "We want to see if you can identify colors without using your eyes."

She tried not to smirk. This was going to be easier than she'd thought. She shut her eyes and wrapped the blindfold around them. Something bumped her chair, and then Garrett's fingers brushed hers, helping to tie a knot, inevitably pulling her hair.

She squirmed into a straighter sitting position and slitted one eye. Sighting straight down through the hollow between her nose and cheek, she could see her "pink frost" fingernails resting on her blue denim lap.

There was a scrape and a thump, and then his wide hand reached into view. She resisted the impulse to clasp it before he clasped hers.

"Just relax," he said. "Let me guide your arms."

Suddenly all she could see was wood grain. He'd drawn her hands inside some kind of box, and now her fingers fumbled with the first card he was giving her through the opposite end.

Faking concentration, she tilted her head. The box fit her forearms as snugly as stocks. All she could see was skin and fake walnut.

"Blue," she guessed through gritted teeth.

"Take your time," Garrett said soothingly. She reckoned his tone meant she was wrong. He put another card into her hand. "It's okay to feel the surface."

She wiped her palm over this card, watching for a telltale reflection on her arm. After a few seconds, she gave up and called it green.

He must have put a dozen cards in her hands, and they might all have been the same color—probably white. If only she could have been alone in the room long enough to pinprick identifying holes in them . . .

"Right," Garrett said, and he whisked off the blindfold along with some of her hair.

She blinked and focused on the box that still held her fast. It strongly resembled the kind Bing used to saw her in half. When Garrett bent to release the latches, his after-shave, a scent hinting of cinnamon, caressed her nose. She stared into the graceful whorl of his left ear.

"How'd I do?" she asked into his ear. "Not so hot, huh?"

"Don't worry about it." Lifting the box and putting it aside, he draped the black blindfold over his sleeve and bowed from the waist. "Where would Madam like to dine tonight?"

"I have to work before and after dinner. So someplace informal." Standing, she worked her shoulder bag into place.

"T-shirt and jeans," he suggested, smartly rapping the color cards on the tabletop to even their edges.

She gave him a Grinchy smile. "Bunny suit."

Watching her exit, Garrett found himself fantasizing about how those hips, sheathed in fur or otherwise, would feel against his palms.

OF COURSE, she didn't wear the bunny suit. She wore a clean white shirt, the denim skirt, and her hair in a topknot that dripped tendrils down the back of her neck. Garrett looked fit and sexy in a herringbone jacket over an open-collared dress shirt. Below the belt, it was jeans and sneakers, as usual. They sat in a nearly deserted dining area at a country-western place called Teddy's. In the next room, a happy crowd stomped around the floor to the live band's rendition of *If Your Phone Don't Ring You'll Know It's Me.*

Kate shoveled salad in time to the music till she noticed Garrett watching her.

"I like women with hearty appetites," he said.

She dabbed daintily at her mouth. "This is delicious."

"Plain garden salad?" he said incredulously.

"My aunts are trying to write a cookbook. The salads I've been getting at home are going to make this year's worst dressed list."

"They aren't happy with standard, family recipes?"

She shook her head and felt another wisp of hair slip free. "The working title of this book is *Cooking Without a License*. Their Daredevil's Food Cake has a mustard sugar icing. They served me Wild Oats Meal for breakfast that tasted like it could give you a hang-over."

He swung his head, laughing. "I'd love to meet them."

"They're your kind of people, all right. Energetic. A little crazy." She glanced up from her fork, sorry she'd said that.

He continued to eat, unperturbed. "How long have you lived with them?"

"Almost ten years. I was going to Oklahoma University, trying to decide what career choice to make, living at home with my folks. And then they died in a car accident. I came to Denver on the spur of the moment, once the estate was settled, just for a visit. You can fill in the blanks." She renewed her attack on the lettuce. "How about you? Besides Ann, do you have relatives in the area?"

"Only Ann, and she doesn't live very close. Boulder." He swallowed some ice water and winked. "Thank goodness." Pushing aside his empty plate, he expanded, "She's a good gal, but she'll always be my bossy big sister. Our parents retired to Florida last year. They owned a drugstore in Aurora while I was growing up."

The waitress interrupted, bearing steaming platters of steaks and vegetables. In anticipation Kate wriggled in her seat.

"So you think I'm crazy, huh?" Garrett said, reaching for the pepper.

Apparently her comment hadn't sunk without a ripple after all. She watched him rock the pepper shaker to the left and then to the right. "Not really out of your mind. Just eccentric," she explained.

"Good. I want to stand out from the crowd." He held up the pepper inquiringly. She was surprised to see that there was actually some left, but she signaled no thanks.

The steaks kept them busy for a few quiet minutes. Kate wanted to ask if he was or had ever been married. Just for the record.

"I haven't shared a one-on-one dinner with a female for a long time," he said, giving her the opening. "This is nice."

"I'll drink to that." She raised her coffee cup and looked at him. "You never married?"

"Too busy—earning a psychology degree in three years—wangling the directorship of CROPS—setting up the lab—walking the dog, washing my hair, stuff like that."

The music next door had slowed to a waltz featuring a fiddle and a male vocalist who sounded as if he was on the verge of tears.

"What was the point of that colors test?" Kate asked.

"Some people really do seem able to sense colors by touch. They claim there's a difference in feel. Like, red's slippery, yellow's grainy—" He noticed she was frowning. "Hey, I can't do it myself."

"What can you do yourself? Did you really use ESP to predict your surprise party?"

"Of course. It wasn't hard. Especially since Ann throws me one every five years."

Kate's expression slipped from rapt attention to relaxed amusement. "Then how does she expect it to be a surprise?"

"Oh, I'm sure it's always a surprise to Ann. I guess she hasn't noticed the semi-decade pattern."

"Like I said," Kate persisted, "what can you do?"

His crinkly eyes warned her he wasn't ready to give a straight answer. "Bake bread, change a tire, translate a little French, read a mind now and then."

"Read any good ones lately?"

He'd probably heard that one before. Instead of laughing, Garrett stared at her intently. Uncomfortable and suddenly feeling superstitious, she dropped her napkin on the floor so that she could hide her face for a moment. She made an effort to blank out Bing and magic, just in case. And all carnal speculations, ditto.

"You're thinking of black velvet," Garrett said and stabbed a potato to show he'd lost interest in the game.

"How'd you know that?" she exclaimed.

"Everyone tries to think of something bland when I announce I can read their private thoughts." He sighed. "All I really do is use common sense and psychology. It's just a trick."

"Oh." She felt oddly sorry.

"All I can do well is uncover other people's paranormal abilities. Theorize. Design experiments. Publicize successes. Expose frauds."

Kate missed her mouth with the fork. "Frauds?" she repeated, wiping steak juice off her cheek.

"Paranormal studies attract a lot of crackpot attention, folks who think they hail from Mars or who believe their neighbors are zombies. Then there are our insecure scientist colleagues whose brains are vapor-locked when it comes to anything supernatural." He made a face at his sip of coffee. "And worst of all are the frauds, the con artists who're just out to make money from the gullibility of others."

Kate joined him in a disgusted shake of the head. Her purse containing Bing's five-hundred-dollar check burned against her hip.

"You and Mac run the whole show yourselves?"

"Pretty much. If we need a third person, for example an objective judge on a test result, we recruit whoever's handy—meter reader, mailman, sales rep. There's a janitor who comes in twice a week and spends more time tabulating test results than he does dusting furniture."

Remembering the state of the lab, Kate thought that went without saying. "Tell me about the test you called remote viewing." She needed more information if she was going to do better than she'd done today.

"Mac goes to some distinctive location within a half hour's radius of the lab. While he looks around and takes photos, the volunteer is trying to receive impressions of what Mac is seeing and then the volunteer describes or draws them."

Kate gazed at her last bite of steak, contemplating loopholes. "Do you know where Mac goes?"

"Nope. That way I can't inadvertently give any hints. And the volunteer can't simply read my mind."

"Simply—right." She knew better than to laugh.

Garrett could see she wasn't much of a psychic. She didn't have the mind-set for it—too skeptical. Still, she was interested and seemed to be willing to learn. And even if she was a washout at the lab, there were definite possibilities for taking advantage of activities totally unrelated to work.

"Dessert?" he offered.

4

IT WAS APPLE PIE *a la mode*. Nothing but basic piecrust, sweetened apples, and plain vanilla ice cream. She ate slowly, partly to make the pleasure last, partly because she was so full. When she glanced up, he gave her an open, relaxed smile. She wondered how such a handsome, desirable male could believe in this Twilight Zone stuff? How could he be so misguided?

"Teaching your houseplants to read," she snickered.

"Oh, yeah." Again the mischievous gleam. "Counting comes next."

"They understand English?"

"And canine."

"Smedley. Are you teaching him how to read, too?"

"Don't be ridiculous. Dogs can't read."

Kate clutched her head, laughing with exasperation.

"I can see you don't believe me about the plants," he chided. "I'll show you. Come on back to my place and see for yourself."

"I have to work, remember?" Earlier that evening, he'd met her at Up and Away. She'd left her car there.

"Afterward, then. How many calls do you have to make? I'll take you."

"Just one call, but I can't let you cool your heels waiting for me, ferrying me around."

"No, really. It couldn't take long, less than an hour, right? And then, you can come up for a drink and a demonstration." He watched her as if he were a kid coveting a toy.

While Kate was trying to make up her mind, the current duet on the bandstand was wailing, "Pleeeeze!"

"Okay," she capitulated, aware that it wasn't on Bing's behalf that she'd agreed.

KATE AND GARRETT SHUFFLED into the corporate office of Up and Away as twilight descended on the streets. The homey, cramped room smelled like duplicator fluid.

"What's an eleven-letter word for flimflam? You ought to know that, Katie," said the voice that greeted them.

Jan Blue, owner/manager, always stayed at her desk until every one of her chicks was accounted for. She didn't look like a worrier; she looked like a five-foot tall Anne Bancroft. But woe to the employee who went home without reporting to Jan that the deliveries had been free of muggers, rapists, or dissatisfied customers.

"Starts with an *S*," she added, twining one short black curl around her forefinger.

The *Denver Post* on her desk had been tortured into a five-by-eight square of crossword puzzle. Tapping cigarette ash into a presumably empty coffee cup, she poised her pen expectantly.

"Skulduggery," Garrett whipped out while Kate was still pondering, staring at the ceiling with one eye shut.

"Spell it," Jan commanded. As Garrett spelled out the word, her ballpoint pen carved the letters into the paper. She looked up, grinning, her black-patent eyes shining with curiosity.

"Jan, this is Garrett Brody. Garrett, this is my boss, Jan Blue."

Jan stretched from her chair to shake his hand. "You playing backup tonight, Garrett?"

"Backup?"

"In case a customer gives me trouble," Kate explained. "Sometimes, if we're leery about a particular delivery situation, the delivery person wears a whistle and has a buddy waiting in the car outside. I've always thought a bad guy could probably strangle me with a whistle chain before I'd get out one peep, so I carry Mace instead."

"Don't let her kid you," Jan laughed. "She just doesn't want to share her commission with a backup person."

"An interesting business you run here," Garrett said. "How old is it?"

"My husband and I started it four years ago. It's been a lot of work and a lot of fun."

Kate sidled toward the back room and its lockers. She needed to change into the bunny suit, but she was afraid to leave Jan and Garrett alone in a conversation that might reveal Kate's real career.

"How many employees do you have?" he asked, gravitating toward the bulletin board where Polaroids of costumed adults and balloon bouquets were pinned haphazardly.

"Not counting me, five."

"That many!"

"Well, yes, but they're all part-time."

Kate went back the way she'd come. She could almost hear the whirring gears of Garrett's inquiring mind as he repeated, "Part-time?"

"My daughter Selma is a student, and so is our one male employee. Doretta sells Amway. Laura paints. And, of course, Kate—"

"Has been sick!" she interrupted. "Garrett, I must have left my billfold on the seat of your car. Would you get it for me?"

As Garrett saluted and exited, Jan turned her attention back to the puzzle.

"Don't mention to Garrett about my being a magician, will you?" Kate stage-whispered across the room.

"Okay," Jan whispered back. "Why not?"

"I want to surprise him. I'm working out a private act to try on him."

"I bet you are," Jan teased. "He's cute."

Before Garrett could return empty-handed, Kate slipped into the bunny outfit, "found" her billfold, and hurried to call off the search that had him on his knees, face nearly touching the floorboard.

As he drove her to her last customer of the day, Garrett turned up his jacket collar and hunkered lower in the seat, grumbling about being seen with a rabbit. She folded her arms and thumped her foot.

KATE SAT CROSS-LEGGED beside Garrett on his neatly made water bed, watching him gently adjust a C-clamp on a philodendron leaf. There were four plants, each in its own clay pot, saucered for drips. They were lined up on a child's redwood picnic beach where an ordinary person would have a nightstand.

Satisfied, Garrett straightened his back and buffed the ears Smedley had thrust into his lap. "This is a galvanometer—it works somewhat like a lie detector device," he instructed. "It measures changes in the electrical currents in humans or, in this case, Fred."

"You named your plant Fred?"

"Fred. Otto. Vern," he said, pointing. "And Flo."

"How do you know that one is female?"

"Just look at her. The sensually curved leaf. The shy, provocative stance in the pot." He leaned across Smedley, pointing at a wire on the floor. "Down here's the recording apparatus."

Craning forward, making the mattress slosh, Kate saw a pen drawing a sluggish line on a winding roll of graph paper.

"Quiet day, huh, Fred?" Garrett unrolled the paper a short way. "Nothing's happened." He turned to leer at Kate. "Yet." As if bestowing blessings, his hands were raised over the vine. "Hey there, fella. How you doing? Got enough water? How's the new leaf coming? Uh-huh, looking good, good."

Kate began to scout the floor for her shoes. The come-up-to-my-place-and-talk-to-my-plants line had seemed like a clever variation of the old etchings ploy. She hadn't expected him to actually babble over them. This was too kooky for her.

Her searching eyes snagged on the graph paper. The pen was swooping now, drawing a mountain range. She blinked.

"How'd you do that?" she wondered, trying to picture how it could be rigged with hidden thread.

"This is my friend Kate. What do you think of her?" The pen hiccuped one molehill.

"Okay," she said. "I see what it's doing, but *what* is it doing?"

"Picking up on my emotions. Or yours. Or Smedley's."

"And all your plants can do that?"

"Well, yeah, but I only have the one galvanometer, so they have to take turns on it. This is Fred's week. They get jealous if I don't give each one equal time. Here." He stretched behind her to collect a handful of flash cards from the bookcase headboard. "This is what I meant by teaching them to read." His breath stirred the hair on her neck.

She took the cards gingerly.

"Read one to yourself over and over for about a minute. Don't let me see it. Shuffle the cards first." He made a blinder out of his open hand.

"What—" She puzzled over the letters *en* printed in red marker.

"They're nonsense sounds, is all. Go ahead."

Feeling vaguely foolish, she concentrated on the card. Before the minute was up, Garrett nudged her and pointed at the graph. A new pattern of zigzags skated across the paper.

"That's *en,*" he translated. "Do another one." He hooked a spiral notebook out from among the vines and began to write in it.

She studied the second card. When he nudged her this time, she couldn't see much difference in what the pen had plotted, but Garrett called it correctly. *"Des."*

"I still don't understand."

"I wanted to see if plants could associate strong emotions with symbols, nonsense words. Definitions are on the backs of the cards."

She flipped the stack over. *Des* stood for "fire." *En* was "cut."

He took the cards from her and tossed them and the notebook aside. "I've spent considerable time," he said, "sitting here concentrating on each syllable, picturing the corresponding activity given on the card. Now, when an impartial observer like you reads the syllables, my conditioned philodendrons recognize them and get all excited. Furthermore, they can differentiate between the cards. The profile they draw on the graph for 'fire' is different from what they draw for 'cut.'" He raised his hands, cuing applause.

"This is creepy," she said. "How can I ever look another salad in the eye?"

He set both feet flat on the floor. "Want a beer?"

Just as Kate untangled one leg over the side, Smedley, recognizing the signs of imminent departure, moved sideways. The resultant collision was taken by the dog as a kick. Whining and overacting, he crawled under the plant table, refusing Kate's profuse apologies. Fred scribbled wildly on the graph.

"Hey," Garrett said. "Hey, guys, it's okay. This is a really a nice lady." He threw out an arm to hug Kate's shoulders into his chest, grinning like a ventriloquist. "See, a nice lady." Then he looked at Kate. "Is it working?" he asked through clenched teeth.

"Fred's gone into cardiac arrest and Smedley's still signaling a technical foul," she gurgled.

"Kate's a good guy." He deposited a noisy kiss on her cheek. "No need to panic." His nose nuzzled into her neck. "Really—" he turned her forty-five degrees "—good" and kissed her mouth.

Kate tingled from earlobe to breastbone. Her lips felt electrified. The heat that rose between their bodies seemed to be coming from somewhere below her waist.

His mouth mumbled against hers, "Stay calm, everyone."

Carefully disengaging herself, swaying without the support of his arms, she patted ineffectually at her hair. "Think they've had enough reassurance?"

He peered in the direction of the graph paper. "One more kiss ought to do it."

He caught her shooing hand, kissed it, and drew her forward. As he bent over her this time, she kept her eyes on the closet mirror behind him, watching the top of her head, amazed that it wasn't smoking.

Eventually he broke off the kiss with a satisfying little twist of his mouth. They shared a sigh. Finally she could pick up her shoes.

"Hmm. Fred registered some new reaction here a moment ago," Garrett said.

She ignored him, tying her laces with fingers that felt like sausages.

"Beer," he said and left her to find her own way to the kitchen.

Like the rest of the apartment, it was small. No windows, two skylights. Cluttered but clean.

Wiping the tops of two beer cans with a dish towel, Garrett snapped the tabs and poured hers into a Garfield mug. "Sorry. All the jelly glasses are in the dishwasher."

He relaxed against the counter, ankles crossed. When he tilted his throat to drink, his shirt tightened across his chest. Wriggling onto a wicker bar stool, she let her eyes brush down his body and was thankful, again, he couldn't actually read her mind.

"How many psychics have you discovered at CROPS?"

Removing Smedley from his toes, Garrett poured a tablespoon of beer into the water bowl by the refrigerator. "We don't discover psychics. It's like musical or artistic ability. We provide the right atmosphere and tools, and they discover themselves."

"Then how many physics have discovered themselves at your lab?"

"Well, we're only a couple years old." He took a final swallow and squeezed the can in his fist.

"None, huh?" She tried to sound sympathetic.

"No, I didn't say that. You can judge for yourself if you're at tomorrow's remote viewing. A couple of other volunteers are scheduled for ten o'clock."

She promised to be there without bells on.

As he walked her to her car, the breeze coming east off the Rockies made her shiver, so he scrubbed her arms for her, hugging her in a brotherly way as they strolled. The final kiss he initiated through the open window of the Honda was brotherly too, till he drew back with a delicate lick to her lower lip, making her shiver all over again.

HANK WAS STILL UP when Kate came into the kitchen at about midnight. The house smelled of boiled cabbage and varnish. It appeared, fortunately, that the latter had been an ingredient in the bunny box, not part of a casserole. The box, drying on the kitchen table, had not yet acquired its secret compartment.

Hank glanced up from her issue of *Popular Science*. "How was the dinner date?"

"Delicious," Kate said. "So was the meal."

Hank giggled. "What's he do for a living?" she asked.

Kate bent over the table to admire the box and waggled her eyebrows. "He's a paranormal research scientist."

"How nice."

"Nice?"

"Clean."

"Clean?"

"Indoor work."

Kate sighed. "Do you really believe in any of that stuff? ESP for example."

"I'm not sure. It's fun to think about."

"Dr. Brody—Garrett—makes it sound like fun. You'd like him."

"Bring him by anytime." Hank propped her chin on her fist and paged through the magazine. "We'll get out the Ouija board."

"When you do meet him, would you please not mention that I'm a magician?"

"Of course I won't," Hank agreed so readily that Kate's mouth, about to explain why not, closed with a click. After a minute of wondering what her aunt thought was wrong with magicians, she asked it out loud.

"Nothing," Hank responded. "Magic is an honorable profession. But does Dr. Brody know that?" Her magazine swished shut like a final curtain.

LATER IN HER MOONLIT BED, eyes fixed on the gleam of the brass footrail, Kate thought about being honorable.

Why should she feel guilty about doing exactly what she'd spent countless hours learning to do? People actually paid her to trick them. Fool the eye. Mystify the mind. Audiences applauded loudest when she was her shiftiest.

Ahh, but Garrett didn't know he was an audience.

She flopped onto her stomach, making the mattress wheeze. He deserved to be fooled. Wasting his life on that outlandish nonsense. She'd be doing him a favor if her subterfuge shamed him into going into some other line of work. She certainly didn't want to waste any more of her own time sparking with a space case like him.

Spark was the word for it, all right.

She closed her eyes but couldn't sleep. Maybe her worrying was pointless. After all, so far she hadn't figured out a way to cheat on a remote view test.

She fell asleep, eventually, by picturing the stereo system she'd buy with the thousand bucks.

5

TEN O'CLOCK WAS ANNOUNCED in the Victorian laboratory, fittingly, with a resonant chime. Kate rocked forward from her gimpy, plastic chair, and shook hands with the other two volunteers as they entered the testing room, a conservatively dressed man and a girl in fluorescent yellow overalls. "Kate Christopher."

"Perry Strickland."

"Nicki Graffman."

Mac peeked in from the hall, jingled his keys at them, and vanished. Garrett hadn't made an appearance yet.

Perry strolled to the farthest corner table and sat, hands folded on it, like a well-behaved pupil awaiting his teacher. He had the detached, defeated air of the school nobody, though it had probably been twenty years since he'd attended school. When Kate asked him if he'd done this kind of test before, he looked past her shoulder and said, "No."

"I've done it lots of times," Nicki announced. She had sat with a thump two chairs away from Kate and tilted it on its back legs. Swinging one arm in a casual pendulum motion, she stuck her tongue out at the observation mirror. "Old Gare is probably in there right now, playing Peeping Tom."

Kate couldn't help staring herself, at Nicki's orange hair. Shaved over the ears, chopped in odd lengths elsewhere, bangs to the bridge of her nose—it was either some stylist's specialty or she'd cut it herself with hedge clippers.

"It's your first time, right?" Nicki asked with faint condescension. "Don't sweat it. Easy street."

"Uh, right. How does Mac decide where to go?"

"Random target. He sticks the name of six kind of distinctive places in envelopes he's numbered one to six. Then he drives off a ways, stops, and throws a die. Whatever number comes up, he opens the corresponding envelope and goes there."

"Are the envelopes safety-lined and sealed?"

"Course. And locked in a file cabinet with a rattlesnake. You know about cheats, huh?" The swinging arm plunged into a pocket and dredged up a stick of gum which Nicki accordioned into her mouth.

"A little." If she could get past the lock and the apocryphal snake, she could squirt a little Freon on the envelopes to make them temporarily transparent, but that still wouldn't tell her which of the six locations the dice would designate.

"Gare don't allow no cheaters around here," Nicki declared. "He even makes his potted plants take lie detector tests."

The twinge of irritation she felt was, Kate had to admit, jealousy. "You've seen his philodendrons?"

"Not in person. But I'm going to baby-sit them when he goes on vacation."

"He's going on vacation?" Kate hoped she sounded polite and not just nosy.

"He never goes on vacation. Unless maybe he did today. He's late enough." Nicki motioned at the one-way mirror to "come on."

This didn't bring Garrett running. Kate leaned past Nicki's profile to include Perry in the conversation. "Have you had some paranormal experiences?"

He frowned at his interlocked knuckles. "Maybe."

Another minute shuffled by before Nicki announced, "There's this lab in Colorado Springs that uses a bunch of computers to test psi. They got games like Volition, where you have to will the cursor line to go up or down." She cracked her gum thoughtfully. "Computers make it harder to cheat."

Kate was considering the possibility of substituting weighted dice for Mac's. The footsteps slamming up the hall could only be Garrett's.

"Drat," Nicki said. "Forgot my pen. You got an extra, Katie?"

She fumbled one out of her shoulder bag and passed it over, anticipating Garrett's handsome face.

"God!" Nicki exclaimed just as he strode into the room. "I can't use this. It's vibrating a minus 6.0 on the Richter scale. I'm talking negative, bad negative vibes."

Garrett passed around good mornings and three particle board screens to fence off each volunteer's section of tabletop.

Nicki made a production out of returning Kate's pen to her, holding it at a distance as if it were rotten and wiping her hand down her thigh once she'd dropped it into Kate's lap.

If Garrett had noticed, he pretended not to, and the ballpoint he handed Nicki at her request seemed to satisfy her. She clicked it twice and leaned back, ready.

Consulting his wristwatch as he distributed blank paper, Garrett said, "Mac's been out twenty-five minutes. That gives me five minutes to discuss the rules for the benefit of our new members. Once the test is underway, there is no talking." It might have been for Kate's benefit, but Nicki was the one to whom he gave a pointed look.

"Please put your name and the date on every piece of paper you use for your psychic impressions. You may write words of description or draw a picture or do both. Do not try to name a particular place. Instead, just write or draw what you see or feel about this place that Mac is visiting. Do not worry if what you see or feel does not seem logical. We are not dealing, here, with the left, reasoning side of the brain, but with the right, intuitive side. Kindly number your first test with—surprise!—number one."

"How many we doing today, Gare?" Nicki asked and blew a pink bubble.

"Two. Fifteen minutes for the first one, a thirty-minute break while Mac goes to the second target, and fifteen minutes of receiving at that location. Anyone have a problem with that?" He gave each person a second chance to speak up. "Good. Any questions? Kate?"

He had been brisk, formal, and impersonal. Now as he let his eyes come to a full stop on her face, they warmed. She stared back, bemused by the sensation of dropping through space, forgetting the question and generating a rustle of impatience from Nicki.

"Uhh, okay then." Garrett twisted his wrist to check the time again. "When I give the word, you should begin by jotting 10:31 a.m. beside the date. Now."

He turned away, drew out the chair, and sat, elbows on knees, contemplating his socks. Lowering her gaze from the crisp hair curling behind his ears, Kate sighed at the white expanse of paper she was expected to fill with her impressions. She peeked sideways. Nicki had covered her face with a splayed hand and was scratching her knee with the other. Perry's upper body had disappeared entirely behind one of the little particle board screens Garrett had brought in earlier. His legs flapped together in a nervous motion.

Kate shifted her eyes back to the accusingly blank paper. What now? She couldn't fake this test, but now she knew what she'd need to fake another day's. There was the Freon in her equipment case at home, and she could go by Bing's shop for the dice.

Hiding her eyes with one palm, she spied on Garrett through her fingers. He had produced a paperback and was absorbed in it, one arm draped over the back of his chair. The tanned wrist and hand dangled gracefully reminding her of a recumbent lion.

Still admiring him, she began to doodle on the waiting paper. She felt the point slip off the edge into the soft tabletop, repositioned the paper, and made a few more marks. Would Garrett's tan go all the way up his arms, onto his shoulders, wrap around his muscular back, slide down his hard chest, taper with his waist into his jeans?

His jaw tightened and, sensing he was about to look up, Kate dragged her eyes down to the test paper. In the scribbles there, the most prominent lines formed a heart with an arrow through it. Guiltily, she crosshatched the heart shape into a rectangle.

"Time," Garrett said, and she gouged the paper with one last stripe.

"Please put 10:45 at the bottom of the paper," he said. "Coffee is available in the kitchen."

Nicki bobbed to her feet and shook her test at Garrett, gesturing him to take it. "I couldn't see a thing. There are some real hostile forces around here today."

Perry folded his paper before surrendering it. He stood beside his chair while the others left the room.

"I don't know about this," Kate said, handing in her drawing and following Nicki into the hall.

The girl stomped toward the back of the house and shoved aside the last door on the east side of the hallway. When Kate arrived a moment later, Nicki was siphoning fragrant coffee from an electric urn. The kitchen had, apparently, been remodeled in the thirties: white cabinets, white stove, white refrigerator, and a buckling green linoleum floor.

Garrett crowded in behind her, touching her elbow in passing, and opened an overhead cupboard to add a box of graham crackers to their break.

"Do you know anything about the people who built this house?" Kate asked, uncomfortably aware of Nicki studying her.

"They were the grandparents of CROPS's benefactor. Made their money in silver," Garrett answered, stirring sugar into his coffee. "Supposedly they located their mine by using a divining rod."

"Your aura's fuzzy," Nicki said, frowning at Kate.

"You can see light around me? Is that what an aura is?" She tried a friendly smile that Nicki deflected with a sternly shaken forefinger.

"If it's fuzzy, it means you're hiding something."

"What's my aura look like?" Garrett asked jovially, trying to draw Nicki's fire.

"Wide. And red, as always, with energy. Hers," she resumed worrying the bone, "is real skinny and full of black spots."

Resisting the urge to brush off her shoulders, Kate screwed in the smile deeper. "Fascinating."

"Kate. Do you want to see the isolation chamber?" Garrett offered.

Any port in a storm. She nodded.

Leaving their cups and stale crackers, Kate and Garrett went to a room opposite Testing. Rising on tiptoe to the window of the door, Kate could see only blackness and her own distorted reflection. *Fuzzy* reflection. Garrett was stabbing a key at the lock.

"We use this when we want absolute peace and quiet," he said.

"Soundproof, huh?" She stepped past him onto a spongy carpet.

The little white room was windowless. Its furnishings were composed of one reclining chair that must have originated in a dentist's office, and some stereo equipment in dire need of dusting. The overhead light wasn't bright enough by which to read, but it sparkled Garrett's hair.

"The floor's mounted on a floating platform so it doesn't pick up vibrations from the rest of the house. Have a seat."

She eased herself into the padded plastic chair, discovered it was more comfortable than it looked, and crossed her ankles on the footrest. "Just trim a little off the sides and top," she joked.

Garrett held up a headphone set, tucked it under his arm, held up a Ping-Pong ball, and showed her it had been cut in half. She thought of Bing, titillating his audience with props before he actually performed the trick.

"Sensory deprivation. Puts you in touch with the real you. These are for your lovely eyes," Garrett said, fitting the half balls gently in place. The light that filtered through was pink and undisturbed by shadows.

"And these are for your lovely ears," he said. He delicately combed her hair back with his fingers before attaching the fat earphones, which whispered faint static.

Kate could feel her "good sport" smile smooth into a natural, tranquil line. Her hands uncurled from the arms of the chair and clasped each other loosely in her lap. She hoped, dreamily, that he would kiss her.

But a moment later, his fingers were in her hair again, lifting away the earphones, then the Ping-Pong shades. Blinking at the light, she swung her knees around and stood up. She hadn't recovered completely from total relaxation, so she stumbled into Garrett's arms. Her neck swung instinctively backward, putting her mouth inches from his.

"Sorry," she lied, and made a token effort to step away.

"The Zephyrs play tonight."

Examining his statement for double entendre, she asked cautiously, "Is that a rock band?"

His coffee-scented breath caressed her cheek as he chuckled. "I can see you're a baseball fan." His open palms scrubbed lazy circles on her back. "I've got two tickets. I suppose you have to work."

She hated baseball. "What time?"

"Starts at seven." His hands gravitated to her upper arms and he set her away from him. "We could go late or leave early or whatever fits your schedule."

"Okay. I'll check it and call you." When he let go, she felt cold on every part of her he'd touched.

They finished their break in the kitchen listening to Nicki's lecture on nonbelievers. "You know how long people were riding in boats before Archimedes discovered the principle of liquid displacement? A long time! We don't have to explain ESP, we just have to ride it."

"Hear! Hear!" Garrett said, thumping his empty cup on the counter by the sink. "Time to go ride some ESP, folks."

They straggled back to the testing room, accepted fresh paper from Garrett, and settled into their chairs. Nicki ostentatiously moved away from Kate to the row behind. Giving the orders to begin, Garrett walked to the window, a dreamy look on his face. Kate poised her pen and waited for inspiration to strike.

Chin on fist, she imagined Mac slamming his car door, camera balanced against his shirt front, walking—where? Sidewalk, probably. She could just hear the grit under his soles, feel the sun on his head. Her doodling hand made six purposeful passes. She drew curved parallel lines. He's at a contour farm field, she thought self-mockingly, and prepared to try again on the lower half of the paper.

Her mind wandered to the problem of the birthday puppy in the box trick. She'd have to do it fast, before the pup had time to struggle and whine and give his secret location away. Maybe a pacifier would keep him happy. She'd need a confederate—an older sibling?—to hand her the dog and the box at the right moment. She was betting one of the neighbors would lend her his little mutt for a dress rehearsal.

With less enthusiasm, she puzzled over the remote viewing trick. How was she going to get hold of the envelopes containing Mac's targets?

Garrett called, "Time," and she twitched back from the edge of sleep.

Gathering up their papers, he said, "If anyone has to leave now, it's okay, but if you want to find out how you did, Mac should be back in about twenty minutes." He stuffed everything into a file folder and bustled out.

All three volunteers stayed, Kate killing the balance of the time by filing her nails, Perry memorizing the ceiling, and Nicki soliloquizing on some esoteric photographic process. Perry yawned, setting off an epidemic, and then Mac's car jounced up the driveway. A few minutes later, he and Garrett entered the room.

Taping their test papers in a row on the wall, primary teacher style, Garrett accepted a handful of photos from Mac to tape below them. Everyone craned forward.

6

USING HIS CAR KEY as a pointer, Mac motioned in the direction of the farthest photo. "This was the first target. Mr. Strickland's got a building shape here, not much else. What happened to you, Nicks?" He twisted to laugh at her over his shoulder. "A blank page?"

"I couldn't see a thing. Something didn't feel right in here today," she grumbled.

"Hey, how about this?" Mac went on, leaning closer to the third test paper. "A star in the making?"

Kate misunderstood the comment and started to confess, "No, it was a heart."

"Very promising, huh, Garrett?" Mac said.

"She's definitely worth watching."

Kate skirted the table and stretched to inspect Mac's photo of a little clapboard church, its pointy steeple at a seventy-degree angle. Her eyes drifted up to her "psychic" drawing with its Cupid's arrow drawn at a seventy-degree angle.

"Uhh, thanks," she said, backing away and fighting down a giggle.

"And over here—" Mac tapped the snapshot of the second target. "The luck of the draw put me at Red Rocks."

He'd photographed the open-air amphitheater from the top row of bench seats. The rusty rock backdrop formed a natural bowl for the stage, beyond which the eastern plains floated in pale blue haze.

Everyone studied Perry's rendering of what could be interpreted as a wide stage or a pond or a large pizza. Then they looked at Nicki's drawing, which was definitely the beer plant in Golden, because it was labeled Coors in bold block letters.

Kate turned away, searching for her purse. Her contour farm field wasn't going to impress Mac.

But she was mistaken. "Wow," he exclaimed. "Look at these lines and look at these along here." Intrigued, she drifted closer to peer over his shoulder.

The curved, parallel lines on her test paper resembled one shot Mac had taken of the tiers of seats. On the bottom half of the paper were ink scratches she couldn't remember making. They resembled the inviting slopes of her graceful brass bed. Or the equally enticing sweep of a theater stage.

Nicki glowered at her, but it was Perry who said, "Could we see the envelopes that contained the snapshots of the random targets?"

Hey, thanks, Perry, I needed that, Kate thought.

Mac retrieved his trusty clipboard from the end of Kate's table and pulled six white envelopes from it. Two had been pried open with a blunt forefinger, the others were still sealed.

Perry raised one of the sealed envelopes toward the light and Kate, squinting with him, concurred that nothing could be read through the blue lining.

She edged closer as he spread out one of the torn envelopes and slipped out a sheet of bond paper folded twice. Unfolded, it displayed part of a line from a pica typewriter that needed a new ribbon: Red Rocks Amphitheater.

"Is it okay if I open one of the remaining envelopes?" Perry asked.

Kate, intrigued by his sudden ability to express himself in complete sentences, found herself wondering why he was interested in the very thing that interested her—the potential for fraud. She leaned with him to examine the sheet of paper that he'd withdrawn from one of the previously unopened envelopes.

"Coors plant," he said.

Nicki groaned as if she'd drawn the wrong card in a game of poker.

While Perry opened the remaining envelopes, showing that the targets were all different, Kate thought of another way that she might be able to cheat. She could use the same kind of paper and typeface, make up six envelopes in advance, all designating the *same* target, and substitute her envelopes for Mac's just before he left the lab. Of course, she'd have to arrange that there be only one test that particular trip out. And that the unopened envelopes be replaced with Mac's again, after the testing.

Engrossed in her scheming, she almost missed Garrett's inquiry. "Would any of you want to try this again tomorrow?"

She and Perry raised their hands. She'd have to arrive early and snoop around to find the target envelopes.

"I don't see any point in my coming in with *this* group," Nicki said pointedly. "When you going to get computers, Gare?"

"When you going to give me a couple thousand dollars, Nick? Computers don't grow on trees, you know." The good-natured bear hug he bestowed to her neon shoulders seemed to cheer her up considerably. "Ten in the morning?" he suggested to Perry and Kate.

WHEN KATE RETURNED TO the Up and Away office from what she hoped was her last singing telegram of the day, Selma was perched on a corner of Jan's desk, her matchstick figure not in the least flattered by the Roman toga she was wearing. Figuring Selma owed her at least one favor, Kate asked her to cover for her on any deliveries that had been scheduled for that night.

"I've been invited to a baseball game by the fella I brought in here last night," she felt obliged to explain to her boss.

Jan smirked and rolled her eyes. "Big date in every sense of the word," she informed Selma. "You should see him."

Selma, whose breathy little voice didn't always do justice to a telegram's lyrics, imitated her mother's brisk alto. "So, Selma, when are *you* going to drag home a husband, preferably your own?"

"Whoa, we're not talking husband yet," Kate protested.

Jan's lighter clicked and smoke gusted as she laughed. "Oh, you will be, I can tell. This is going to get serious. I've got a sixth sense that says so."

Selma stretched her scrawny arms above her fashionably frizzy hair. "I'll do your calls tonight, Kate, if you name the first kid for me."

"Sorry. I don't think he'd like having a girl's name."

"Oooo-kay. I'll do it anyway," Selma conceded, slipping off the desk to go change costumes. She gave Kate one of the spontaneous, surprisingly strong hugs that gave her character such an endearing quality.

"Play ball," she advised.

MILE HIGH STADIUM WAS PERHAPS a quarter full. Garrett's red wooden seats faced first base where a spraddle-legged Zephyr nervously smacked fist to mitt awaiting the top of the sixth in a scoreless ball game. Kate sipped a soft drink, watching the white moon arc above the bleachers across the field. It had a fuzzy aura.

"Is Nicki clairvoyant?" she asked.

"What?" Garrett was distracted by the crack of ball on bat and the pounding of the players' feet.

"Nicki. Can she usually remote view?" Kate winced as the runner threw himself feetfirst at the baseman.

"Better than chance," he answered. His "Yeah!" was for the umpire's call that sent the runner limping back toward the bull pen.

"How about Perry?" She wondered, again, why she'd agreed to come to a stupid baseball game.

But Garrett made it all worthwhile. "I don't know," he answered. "Today was his first test session."

"What does he do for a living?"

"He's a private eye. Steeerike!"

"A private—no kidding? That quiet little man?" Chewing ice chips from the otherwise empty cup, she tried to picture Perry whipping a gun out of his armpit and yelling "Freeze!"

"You've heard of psychics assisting the police? He hopes to develop whatever paranormal talent he has, to help him in his investigations. Want another cola?"

"No, thanks."

What she wanted was to go home. Just then his arm dropped across her back, hand on shoulder, and she figured she could stick it out a little longer. She could even clap for the last strike that retired the side.

While she watched the game, she thought about the things she still had to do tonight or first thing in the morning. Like type the name of a target—the same name, six times—and seal it in envelopes identical to Mac's. Trying to think how to limit the test to one target, so that Mac wouldn't open another envelope and find it a duplicate, Kate visualized another problem.

"Who thinks up the target sites and prepares the test envelopes?"

"Mac, usually." A foul tip took his mind off the peculiar timing of the question.

If Mac prepared the sites, he would surely recognize one he hadn't included. Maybe she'd better go back to plan A, the weighted dice for ensuring Mac picked a certain envelope, and Freon to make the envelope temporarily transparent for her to read what it contained.

Of course, like plan B, this scam didn't give her an opportunity to be brilliant two targets in a row. Even if she could weight the die two ways, she couldn't be sure in what order the two targets would come up. Maybe just as it had happened today, she grinned to herself, coincidence would make her look good.

Garrett's voice was loud against her ear. "Why all the shoptalk?"

"Because I don't know any baseball talk?" she suggested.

He ripped his arm away to applaud a hit into deep center field, and Kate empathized with the little boy two rows down who put his bored face into his dad's shoulder and went limp.

The Zephyrs won, four to nothing. Having spent the last few minutes of the game composing a pretty little refusal speech to use when Garrett invited her up to his place for a beer, Kate felt mildly indignant when he took her straight home without offering her an opportunity to recite it.

He did, however, walk her to the door, take her in his arms, and kiss her with the concentration of someone embarking on a long, potentially hazardous, trip. When he freed her and started towards the car, she considered tagging him and asking him for an instant replay.

SHE FOUND CORLISS AND HANK washing up their supper dishes. Kate puzzled over the assortment which included a roasting pan, two fondue forks, and a nutcracker, but she didn't ask for an explanation. She did ask, however, if they thought Mr. Bledsoe up the street would let her put his dog Pepper through a trial run in the bunny box; they assured her he'd consider it an honor.

"You're home early from your date," Corliss observed. "You didn't have a fight, did you?"

"We'll see each other tomorrow," Kate reassured her.

"Is this the supernormalist or whatever he is? The ESP doctor?"

"Yup. You're going to love him. He talks to his houseplants. And they pay attention, too."

"We should ask him about telepathy," Hank and Corliss said in unison, raising their eyebrows and laughing.

"I have to run downtown to the magic shop," Kate announced, grinning, one foot poised on the hall threshold. "Anything I can bring you?"

"A rubber chicken?" Hank suggested.

"Isn't the shop closed while Bing's out of town?" Corliss said more to the point.

"You doubt that the great Kathy can get into a locked building?" Kate shot out her sleeves, flashed her bare hands, and plucked a key out of thin air.

"Isn't it awfully late to be running around by yourself?" Corliss fretted. "What is it that can't wait till morning?"

"Dice. And I'll be fine."

"Dice," Corliss snorted and shook her head. "Risking a traffic accident, rape, and not enough sleep for dice."

Like Kate, Hank imagined she could cope with any of the above. She smiled sympathetically. "Be careful," she said, largely for Corliss's benefit.

And it *was* a trifle spooky, letting herself into the shadowy shop from the deserted, lamplit Sixteenth Street promenade. The bell on the door gave a gentle, token tinkle as she slipped through and locked it behind her.

The floor-to-ceiling merchandise, so garish and glittery in daylight, huddled gray and ghostly in the weak night-light Bing felt he could afford. Random words on box lids and book spines leaped out at her: Flash, Floating, Torch, Voodoo, Noose, Snake, Blade. A pungent mixture of incense, sulphur, and Bing's cigarettes permeated everything.

Drawing aside the door of a glass case, Kate grabbed one each of every color trick die, not knowing what color Mac's might be, and rustled them into a brown paper sack. On a scratch pad by the phone, she printed in big block letters, "Bing: IOU rental on 17 dice unless I can sneak them back where they belong before you get home from Vegas." She signed it "Womandrake," grinning at how irritated he'd be if he did get back first. Locking up afterward, she heard the grumble of distant thunder and felt theatrically sinister.

AT THAT MOMENT it was raining softly on Garrett's kitchen skylights. He sat at the counter, iced tea in one hand and pen in the other, writing a book review for one of the professional journals that hired him to do this in exchange for a copy of the book. He'd put it off too long this time; it had to go into the mail tomorrow for sure. And so he hadn't been able to invite himself in at Kate's when he wanted to prolong the evening.

He tossed the pen down, irritated to find himself playing hooky again, thinking of Kate instead of about "differential electrical potential between front and back brain in ESP subject testing." Standing and stretching, he gave in completely to the temptation of picturing her sunny face and energetic body.

"Special," he told an attentive Smedley, hovering hopefully by the refrigerator. "It may not be ESP, but she's got *something*. When's the last time I said that about a woman?"

The dog, excited to be noticed, barked once.

"Seventh grade? Come on, Smed! You and I didn't know each other then." Garrett shared a handful of peanuts before getting back to business.

ON WEDNESDAY MORNING Kate arrived at the lab forty-five minutes early and was pleased to find only Mac's car in the parking lot.

"Hello," she called, stepping through the back door. The distant patter of typing seemed a good omen. Touring the lower hall, she quietly opened doors till the one marked Supplies stubbornly stood its ground. She even peeked through the old style keyhole, but all she could see was a few inches of scratched, black cabinet.

Records was also locked. Testing stood wide open but was forbiddingly bare, no test papers decorating the wall. The sporadic typing continued to sift down from upstairs.

Tiptoeing up the steps was impossible; they creaked and crackled like fresh cereal. At the top, she called again, "Hello."

"In the office," Mac answered.

He hunched over the massive, antique Underwood typewriter, using two fingers to peck out the letters. "You're early."

"Yeah. I didn't have car trouble," she wisecracked, craning to see over his shoulder.

Before she could read anything, he fell across the typewriter, arms protecting its paper tongue. Frantically, he freed one hand to overturn a little stack of pages on the desk.

"Out! Out! You'll contaminate the test controls. Wait in the hall."

"Oh. Sorry."

As soon as she'd cleared the threshold, he jumped up and slammed the door in her face. "Go get yourself a cup of coffee," he yelled.

On the way back to the staircase, she quietly tried to open more doors. All of them opened, but none of the rooms yielded anything helpful. Beginning to feel thwarted, she went downstairs and into the sun-striped kitchen, where the coffeemaker was softly belching to itself.

Siphoning off two cups, she retraced her way up to the office, arms at an awkward, don't-spill angle. Outside the closed door, she listened to the absolute quiet before calling out brightly, "I brought you some, Mac."

The quiet lingered a moment longer. Then a drawer slammed and shoes hit the floor. The door opened wide enough for one hand to accept the coffee.

"Thanks," he said without enthusiasm. "Sorry, but you'll have to wait in Testing."

"Gee, I was hoping to see how you set up the remote viewing. For example, where do you get your ideas for targets. How do you choose the actual place to go? Dice?"

Mac widened the crack just enough to slither through and shut the door behind him. "We have to keep tight control of the testing procedure or we leave ourselves open to charges of fraudulent results. I can't let you see anything right now. Maybe you'd like to ride along some day when you aren't being the receiver."

Her shoulder bag with its added weight of dice and Freon canister slumped to the floor as Mac pulled himself back into the office and firmly shut the door. There was the unmistakable snick of a key, rudely underlining her rejection.

Kate shuffled toward the stairs, wondering how she would kill the next thirty minutes.

7

"THIS MUST BE THE PLACE" someone blared, knocking Kate's chin off her supporting hand, thumping her knee against the underside of the table, and clicking her eyes fully awake.

The man blocking the doorway of Testing beamed at her. He was carrying a cane. His body was square-shaped. A box with a head on top. Complexion the color and texture of well-worn leather. White hair cropped down to the stubble. His crow-black eyes ricocheted around the room and finally settled on Kate.

"You going to see what you can see?" he asked her.

She smiled and nodded, and, as if this gesture constituted an invitation, he lumbered into the room.

He used his cane to push aside chairs and to point. "That seat spoken for?"

"Now it is," she said, holding on to the smile for Perry Strickland who was just entering the room. Not taking any notice of Kate's greeting, he took the same place he'd occupied the previous morning.

"How often have you been here, miss?" the newcomer inquired.

He'd chosen to sit a couple of chairs down from Kate. She wondered if she should warn him about her aura.

"This is my second time. How about you?"

"Never. Another new adventure in an otherwise full life." He rubbed his jaw. "What's this Dr. Brody like? Smart, is he?"

"Very. Bubbling over with ideas." She stretched her arm across the backs of the chairs, offering her hand. "I'm Kate Christopher."

"Pleased. Rudy Garcia." He looked her hard in the eyes before he let go of her hand. "Are you pretty smart, too?"

"About some things." She could see he was one of those senior citizens who had no qualms about being direct because life was getting too short for subtleties.

"I know you're smart, just looking at you. Very attractive, too. Do you think there's any way Brody could be falsifying his test results?"

Kate's mouth flopped open. "Falsifying—" Her eyes refocused to Perry sitting beyond. "No, I'm sure he wouldn't—"

"How about someone else tricking him?" Mr. Garcia's expression was how she'd always imagined "inscrutable" would look.

"No. Why do you ask?" she said, kicking her incriminating shoulder bag further under the table.

"I'm new at this parapsychology stuff. I want to know if it's real or a lot of hooey."

"There are a lot of people who'd like to know that," she said solemnly. It bothered her that Perry hadn't been included in the conversation. "That gentleman there is—"

"I know," Mr. Garcia interrupted, just short of being rude. "So you haven't noticed anything to indicate carelessness, unprofessionalism?"

"Oh, no. They keep everything under lock and key," she assured him wryly.

At that moment Garrett rushed in. It took a full minute for Kate to compose herself so that his words of welcome and instruction could begin to register. She accepted her screen and blank paper unenthusiastically, feeling as if she were a failure at magic about to become a failure at ESP. The touch of Garrett's hand on hers as he turned to give Mr. Garcia his supplies was the best thing that had happened to her all morning.

The test time began, and Kate, yawning, penned a sun shape in the left-hand corner, a row of mountains or trees, and—she might as well fail creatively as well—a bear in the lower right-hand corner. This accomplished, she indulged in surreptitiously watching Garrett.

Seated with his right ankle on his left knee in an exclusively male posture, Garrett was wearing a pale blue dress shirt, the collar brushing his jaw as his head bent to read the book in his lap. His thumb and finger held and gently abraded the page he was about to turn, and Kate shuddered reflexively. Startled and embarrassed, she laid her head on her arms and tried to think of black velvet.

During the break between tests, she invited Garrett to supper.

"Who's doing the cooking?" he asked suspiciously, working his hip onto the edge of her table. The others had gone to find coffee.

"Tonight's my aunts' bingo night. They'll be gone from six to eleven." As her smile grew, he matched it, tooth for tooth.

"Don't you have anything better to do?" he said. "I mean, this will be three nights in a row. You're not just feeling sorry for me, are you?"

"Sorry?" She pretended to give it some thought. "No, that isn't it." She straightened his already straight collar. "Want to guess again?"

His hand covered hers, pressing it into his chest, and his heart thrummed against her fingertips. Still grinning, he slowly lowered his head and gave her the kiss she'd been yearning for. Warmth uncurled in her belly. She wound her fingers in the cloth of his shirt, holding him close for a while.

Voices and shoes echoed in the hall. Mr. Garcia's cane punched an unmistakable counterpoint.

Garrett drew away as if it were an effort. "Six o'clock," he said.

"Don't bring Smedley or Fred," she requested sweetly.

The others entered the room and took their places in preparation for the next test.

During the second test period, Kate decided to use words instead of pictures. "Park bench," she wrote. "Water. People walking around. Bushes and trees." When she finally got tired of doing this, she used another piece of paper to make a grocery list.

When Mac arrived, the test papers and photos were posted as they had been the previous day. Mr. Garcia, who had apparently been even less inspired than Kate, had marked a large *X* on his paper. Perry had done a very good likeness of Santa Claus. Neither these impressions nor Kate's mountain range came anywhere close to resembling Mac's photos of a Safeway store.

Collectively sighing, the group turned its attention to the second target. Mr. Garcia had drawn a slightly smaller *X*. Perry had drawn a four-legged something. Kate saw that Mac had photographed the interior of a mall. She hadn't really expected it to be her park.

"Again, she's impressive," Mac said.

"Right," Kate said, snickering at his sarcasm.

"Plants. Water. People. Benches. All accounted for."

She took a second look under his elbow at the mall scene. "Right," she repeated.

Mr. Garcia narrowed his eyes and pursed his mouth at her. Beyond him, Perry crossed his arms and rocked on his heels.

"Hey, this is fun," she blurted. "Maybe I'll wear a head scarf and hoop earrings and join a traveling carnival."

THE SINGLE RED ROSE he'd brought her graced the center of the kitchen table in a cut glass vase that was usually used as a vinegar cruet. Garrett and Kate spooned chocolate pudding into their mouths, the delicious finale to a meal of potato soup, tossed salad, sourdough bread, and applesauce.

"I could learn to be a vegetarian," Garrett said obligingly.

"There was supposed to be pork chops, but I burned them," Kate confessed. "I can still smell it."

"I thought the smell was a result of something your aunts had been inventing."

They occupied one corner of the table, seated at right angles to each other, and her foot bumped his. "Sorry."

"My pleasure." Grinning, he licked his upper lip.

"We could've eaten in the dining room, but that's for company."

"I'm honored, not to be company."

After a moment of companionable swallowing, Kate said, "Your security measures at the lab are impressive."

"Shoptalk again?" he appealed, his eyes rolled up to the ceiling. Scooping out the last dollop of pudding in his bowl, he added, "We have to be very careful. Loose lips sink ships. Or in this case, sloppy experiments shoot down our chances for grant money."

"You need money, huh?" She thought of a thousand dollars slowly sinking on her own horizon.

"We always need money. Like Nicki says, we need computers. And fresh graham crackers."

Without asking him if he wanted it, she poured him a third cup of coffee.

"Thanks. I love my job, but I hate having to scrounge for funds, groveling at corporation or government offices that might be able to help."

"Your benefactor's legacy—"

"Is fading fast." He mourned it for a moment. "But, hey, let's not think about that. Bring on the dancing girls. Drink up. Or down, if you prefer."

"No, wait a minute. I have another question." She pushed back her bowl so she could fold her arms on the tabletop. "What if you did have to close the lab? Where would you look for a job?"

"Somebody else's parapsychology research program," he answered promptly. "I'm not proud."

"Yes, but aren't there more opportunities in other branches of science on psychology? And better money?"

"Listen." He beckoned her toward a shared confidence. "Fantastic paranormal discoveries are almost in humankind's grasp. I think I'm going to prove something wonderful before I die. Money would be nice, but I'll settle for worldwide adulation."

She dropped back in her chair, cheeks puffed out in exasperation. She realized she couldn't save him if he didn't want to be saved.

"Speaking of adulation," he said, deliberately nudging her knee with his, "I admire your cooking, your flare for ESP, and the shape you give a pair of jeans. Not necessarily in that order."

"And I admire your zest for knowledge, your way with plants, and the shape you give a pair of jeans. Order to be announced."

He reached along the table to trap her resting wrist and haul it toward him. "I like your collarbone."

She had to stand up to follow her arm around to his side of the table. "I like your sense of humor."

He drew her onto his lap and transferred his grip to the nape of her neck. "I like your trusting nature," he said in a Transylvanian accent.

"I like your trustworthiness," she threatened him back.

"I think I like the way you kiss. Mind if I refresh my memory?" His forehead touched hers in affectionate affirmation.

"Please," she said, as if he'd offered to warm up her coffee.

The kiss was as soft and sweet as summer rain, but it gradually roughened toward lightning and thunder. Garrett's hand trailed down her backbone and on the return trip tunneled inside her shirt. His other hand swam through her hair, cupped the back of her head, and gently held it, tightening the fit of their mouths.

Arms crossed behind his neck, Kate watched colors bloom inside her eyelids, oil in water iridescent, red predominant. She felt the oil slide through her, coat her with a warm, wet glow. It swirled in the pit of her stomach, inched deeper, down between her legs. She sighed and licked chocolate from the corner of Garrett's mouth.

"Kate," he said without taking his lips from hers. "I'm hungry."

Suddenly weak, she shook her head free, fumbled behind herself for Garrett's hand, and forced it around against her chest. Together they tugged her shirttail loose from her jeans to give his fingers entrance to her bare skin. Leaving a track of fire, his hand caressed up her rib cage, found the front hook of her bra, and thumbed it open. She moaned with anticipation and fastened her teeth to his neck. His knuckles brushed the underside of one breast and began, with excruciating slowness, to move higher.

"Yoo-hoo, we're home!"

That, and the bang of a door, jerked them apart like the snap of a hypnotist's fingers breaking a trance. Wrestling her shirt into place, Kate hurriedly left Garrett's lap and collapsed into her own chair.

"In the kitchen," she called breathily.

Hank paused to knock on the doorjamb before Corliss pushed her through. "We won't bother you," she said, unaware of the irony.

"You're home early," Kate said as cheerfully as she could under the circumstances.

"They ran out of bingo prizes early tonight," Corliss said, unabashedly staring at Garrett.

"Well, that's because the wind blew them away. Hi, I'm Hank and this is Corliss, and you're Dr. Brody."

"Garrett. The wind blew them away?"

"Pastor Gimble was trying to carry too much, including Mrs. Gimble. Would you like an after-dinner mint, Garrett? Homemade."

"Thanks, no. Kate's got me ready to explode."

Kate bit her thumbnail and tried to think pure thoughts.

Garrett, who'd scrambled to his feet when the aunts had come in, waved at the table. "Won't you sit down with us and explain why Pastor Gimble was behaving so strangely?"

Corliss and Hank took two steps backward, waving their hands and heads at him. "We won't intrude," one said.

"You'd probably prefer to be alone," the other one decided.

"But if you really want to know," Corliss added, "the pastor was trying to save as much as he could from water damage."

Kate glanced at the window over the sink where twilight, stars, and a clear sky were in evidence. "Water?"

Corliss pursed her mouth. "You know how careless firemen can be."

"The building caught fire," Garrett guessed wildly.

"Only Claire Shively's part of the building," Hank corrected. "She chain-smokes. Such a disgusting habit. And she thinks she can keep twelve bingo cards going all at the same time."

"Come on, Hank. We'll read in our rooms and let the young people have the rest of the house." Corliss disappeared into the hall.

"So in the excitement of getting a bingo, Claire put her marker in the ashtray and her cigarette on a bingo card," Hank said, following Corliss. "It was wonderful. Except they made everyone go home early."

Corliss wandered back into view. "Kate, maybe Dr. Brody would speak to the ficus in the living room about leaf dropping." She led Hank out of sight.

"Nice to meet you," Garrett raised his voice toward the empty doorway.

Hank's last words floated around the corner. "Mr. Bledsoe says you can borrow his toy terrier any time, dear."

Garrett and Kate exchanged the dazed smiles of accident survivors. He found his way back to his chair.

"You need to borrow a dog?"

"Uhh, I thought I'd see if I liked it well enough to get one of my own."

"Smedley's available."

"He's too big."

"Big?"

"Old!" she hastened to correct. "I'm thinking of a puppy."

His fingers walked over the table, up her arm, and across her shoulders to coax her closer. She yearned forward, mouth all set for the taste of his kiss.

Directly overhead a shoe dropped, and Garrett paused till the second sounded. As he resumed his progress, a third thump initiated a series of ceiling-jarring noises.

"What's she doing?" Garrett whispered.

"Jogging in place," Kate whispered back.

"Like me. Getting nowhere fast," he said, completing the kiss.

SHE COULDN'T DO IT. In her cool and very empty bed, Kate made up her mind that night. No cheating. Goodbye thousand dollars. It was too hard, faking results in Garrett's carefully planned lab experiments.

But mostly she was giving up the money so she could seduce him with a clear conscience.

8

FOR A BREAK IN THE ROUTINE, she rode with Mac to the two target spots on the following Thursday. He let her throw the die and open the envelopes that sent them first to an elementary school yard and then to a cemetery. While Mac studied the sites with a keen eye and his camera, Kate tried a swing in the school yard then sat on a stone wall in the cemetery, being careful not to think of Garrett stroking under her clothes, in case any of the volunteers were tuned in to her.

When she and Mac returned to the lab, Perry, Nicki, and Mr. Garcia had *received*, but not loud and clear. Mr. Garcia's drawing of a nude lady gave Kate a turn, till she realized it was one of several statues that had not been in the cemetery and very definitely had not been in the school yard.

Afterward, Garrett invited Kate to lunch—which turned out to be packed in a brown paper bag and contained an apple, a handful of potato chips, and three carrot sticks. Tapping into the coffee urn, he suggested they could supplement their meagre lunch with graham crackers.

"Since you didn't seem delighted with that idea, we could have an early supper, you and I," he offered as an alternative. "Just the two of us."

"That lets out my place," she said, scrupulously halving the extra carrot stick.

"My place then? I won't burn the pork chops."

"What about Smedley and the green quadruplets?"

"I won't burn them, either. I know—that's not what you meant."

They continued to banter quietly, laughing, Kate feeling mellow with her decision to abandon Bing's cause. Sometime she really would have to confess to Garrett about that. But not yet. Not now and not here, where there were too many chances of being interrupted.

She'd no sooner had that thought than a young man with black, bushy hair and a mustache to match, sauntered into the room and let his aluminum bucket clank to the floor. The yellow-handled mop sprouting out of it slumped against the man's chest, and he embraced it casually.

"I can wait," he said, cocking the other hand on his waist and fixing a blank gaze on Kate.

"Joe. Is this Thursday already? I've got three days of remote viewing results for you to judge."

"Suits me. I can always wash the kitchen floor."

Giving the linoleum a sidelong glance, Kate thought his "always" should have been "never."

"Let's go up to the office. Kate, Joe. Joe, Kate." Garrett knocked back the last of his coffee and wadded the brown bag.

Kate wasn't sure if she was really invited to tag along upstairs with them, but in any case, she had telegrams to sing and dogs to materialize. She stood up and gave an affectionate squeeze to Garrett's biceps.

"Gotta go to work. What time tonight?" she asked, trying to ignore Joe's continued interest in her. His head swiveled toward Garrett, as if he were watching a tennis match.

"Oh, okay. Six twenty-seven?"

"Maybe we better synchronize our watches," she said, laughing at Garrett's dry sense of humor.

Seeing the wastebasket was already overflowing, Garrett screwed the lunch bag tighter and tapped it into his shirt pocket. "It shouldn't be any harder to be punctual at odd times than at the traditional half-hour increments."

According to the back and forth movements of Joe's head, it was her turn to speak. She hit into the net. "See you at 6:27 sharp."

Letting herself out the backdoor, she heard the janitor's elated, "Cheee-wah-wah, Doc."

MR. BLEDSOE AND HIS toy Manchester Pepper lived two doors north of Kate's aunts. In this neighborhood of staid, two-story, neutral-colored clapboards, Mr. B.'s flamingo stucco stuck out like a sore, pink thumb. Inside it was homey, knotty pine and sailcloth prints, and there was a blue bottle collection sparkling in the south window that gave Kate the sensation of walking into a swimming pool.

A retired railroad man, Mr. Bledsoe was hard of hearing but an old softy otherwise. Built like a balding teddy bear, he considered his small menagerie family.

Besides Pepper, there was a white cat—called Salt, of course—a parakeet, and a trio of caged gerbils.

Mr. B. helped her move a gateleg table away from the wall to use as a work space. Pepper paced between their feet, obviously suspicious that something unusual was planned. Stooping, Kate scuffed his chin, and he looked at her warily, the whites of his eyes predominant.

Unobtrusively, she covered Pepper's ears so she could yell at Mr. B. "Why don't you sit there on the couch and see if I can mystify you?"

He settled on the edge of the upholstery, hands on knees, ready to spring into a standing ovation.

"Come on, Pepper," she coaxed, lifting the bunny box she'd brought with her while she showed him a piece of kibble for reward. "Let's go into the next room a second, huh, Pep?"

Interested in spite of himself, he trotted out with her. Out of sight of their audience, she scooped him up, palmed the treat into his mouth, and lowered him into the wedge-shaped secret compartment.

If Mr. B. had been beside or behind her as she walked back to the table, he'd have seen Pepper's head between Kate's chest and the open box lid. She tilted the box slightly to show him it was empty, quietly shushing Pepper, who'd decided he'd sold his soul too cheaply. As the dog gathered his legs to leap out, she shut the box lid, simultaneously swinging the secret compartment into the false back.

Pepper, completely inside the box now, yipped, "It's dark," or "Too tight," but Mr. B. couldn't hear. Perhaps a group of hyperactive preschoolers wouldn't be able to hear, either.

"Homestretch, Pep," she encouraged, displaying the box's outsides from every angle to Mr. B.

He grinned and nodded politely, but when she whipped open the lid and Pepper exploded out, the old man clapped with unreserved delight.

"Do it again," he insisted.

Since Pepper had galloped and skidded under the couch and wouldn't be sweet-talked out, Kate used each of the gerbils once, and even Salt, who demonstrated she'd learned the routine from her predecessors, holding quite still till the lid lifted, then leaping out gracefully, and even deigning to accept a kibble reward.

"I still don't know how you do it," Mr. B. marveled.

"Good." Kate couldn't resist pinching his cheek. "I only hope the birthday puppy is as cooperative as your zoo."

THE REST OF THE AFTERNOON she spent for Up and Away, buzzing around Metro Denver in her little red car, making people happy or embarrassed with her songs and costumes. The last call was at five o'clock, and she cursed the rush hour as she fought to get home in time for a shower before going to Garrett's.

As she bounded upstairs to the bathroom, Hank hailed from the kitchen, "Mr. Bing phoned. The number's on the refrigerator."

"Okay, I'll catch him later." *Checking up on his investment*, she thought, ripping off her T-shirt and staggering loose from her jeans. *Wait till he hears how fast the enemy won me over.*

Turbaning her hair with a towel, she dashed into and out of the shower spray. Her selection of clean clothes made her blush. They included her best underwear and a yellow shirtdress that was easy to unbutton from neck to hem....

CHAMBER MUSIC WAS PLAYING on Garrett's stereo. His kitchen smelled of garlic bread, and the dinette alcove was candlelit.

"Perfect," Kate said, as she looked around.

"And you're right on the stroke of twenty-seven." He took her hand and swung it gently between them, like a shy schoolboy.

"I didn't have time to get you a rose, so I brought you a balloon." It was emblazoned with a golden happy face.

"Lovely. I'll get a vase."

Kate chuckled. Smedley had trotted beside Garrett to answer the doorbell, but seeing it was Kate, he slunk back to the bedroom.

"I said I was sorry," she protested.

"Smedleys never forget. You should never kick a Smedley."

Kate pinched kibble up from the bottom of one pocket and bent to offer it. "Would a Smedley stoop to taking a bribe?"

The only stooping he did was to get underneath the plant table.

"Never mind. *I'm* glad to see you." Garrett rubbed an affectionate palm up and down her forearm, and her whole body tingled in response.

He wined and dined her in the south-facing window as the sky hoarded clouds for a summer storm. By dessert—Neapolitan ice cream to crown an all-Italian menu—a presumptuous wind was rapping at the windows. Smedley came out of hiding long enough to roll his eyes at Kate.

"I had nothing to do with it," she called after him.

The yellow-gray sky boiling outside made their dimly lit niche especially cozy. They leaned across the table to each other as if fortunes were being told, the fluttering candle flame highlighting their cheekbones and eye sockets. A scattershot of hail peppered the window, and lightning stitched sky to ground.

"You look magical," Garrett murmured, lacing his fingers through hers.

Ignoring this natural cue to the confession she must eventually make, Kate said only, "And you look marvelously mysterious."

"You're terribly tempting." His thumb massaged her wrist. "And abundantly alluring."

"Disgustingly desirable," she said for her turn. "Stupefyingly sexy."

Slowly unfolding to his full height, he handed her around the table edge into his arms. His cheek rested on her hair while they slow-danced to a Boccherini minuet.

Toes catching in the carpet, Kate half shut her eyes and savored the strength of his arms supporting her as he danced her around the floor, aimlessly at first, and then ever closer to the bedroom doorway. The record faltered in a power surge, sounding like all the instruments had dozed and then wakened together.

"Better shut it off," Garrett muttered, as thunder trembled in the distance.

He snapped switches, hugging Kate with one arm, and steered her to the table again to blow out the candles. In the psychedelic flicker of intermittent lightning, his expression turned from mischievous to serious, his eyes alternately glittering and evasive.

Kate wanted the reassurance of his voice, to be sure it was still Garrett who bent her backward on his arm and rested his free hand on her throat. "You're the most exciting man I've ever delivered a telegram to," she said.

"Is this the same word game?" His voice did sound its familiar, teasing self, but the impression of lurking danger didn't change.

The storm was part of it, heightening suspense as his face slowly descended toward hers. The touch of his warm mouth intensified the turbulence building inside her. While the kiss both soothed and scorched, Kate clung to Garrett's shoulders as if he were rescuing her from peril. Longing intensified to mindless need.

Sliding his mouth sideways, leaving a damp stripe across her cheek, he murmured, "Do you want to lie down as much as I do?"

"Yes," was all she could manage.

Still clinging to each other, they crossed to the bedroom, and Garrett pushed the door wider. The growl it made along its track segued into another growl somewhere near Kate's ankles. The effect was definitely sobering.

"Come on, Smed," Garrett scolded in a gutteral tone, "stop it." Turning to Kate, he added, "Shade your eyes. I'm going to put on the light and put out the dog."

The wall switch clicked, but no light came on. "Seems the power's off," he explained unnecessarily.

He guided her to the edge of the bed. "Sit here. I'll be right back. Come on, Smed. Where are you?"

Lightning revealed Garrett on his knees, reaching under the plant table. "Shh, Fred, it's okay. Smedley, old friend, I'm going to wring your neck," he threatened wryly.

Thunder shook the building, and Smedley yelped. The storm quieted temporarily, but Smedley didn't. While Garrett was alternatively cajoling and cursing, trying to silence and/or capture the hysterical dog, Kate hugged her legs to her chest, striving mightily to hang on to her romantic mood.

"Does he always act like this in a thunderstorm?" she asked.

"No. He's—ouch—just trying to—dammit—get attention."

"It's certainly working," she shouted, trying to cover the deafening sound of hail on the roof.

Smedley's yipping trailed into the hallway, and Garrett smacked the door shut. Although he was breathing hard as he returned to the bed, she doubted it had anything to do with sexual desire.

"He'll settle down. The storm's passing over," he said, patting across Kate's knee to get his bearings in the darkness. "We'll just talk a while, till he gives up."

She rode a wave as he dropped onto the water bed. "He won't. He just doesn't like me."

"That's okay. I like you enough to make up for it. And quite a bit left over."

Kate shut her eyes on the dark, gently rocking room, willing herself to relax and Smedley to shut up. Garrett's hand groped up her arm and tugged her down to lie full-length beside him on the undulating mattress.

Garrett cleared his throat. "What shall we talk about?"

"Anything except baseball. And dogs."

He laid a casual hand on her waist. "Since you seem interested in my work—"

She felt him fumble a button out of its hole. When his palm skimmed inside against her bare midriff, she imagined the touch tanning her, leaving the outline of long fingers for her to admire tomorrow in the mirror.

"Joe matched your test papers to the correct targets ten percent above chance probability," he said with low matter-of-factness.

Finding it difficult to make conversation while Garrett's fingers walked into the waistband of her half-slip, Kate managed to get out, "Is that good?"

"Very. Unless, of course, you cheated."

"No, I didn't cheat." Smedley's claws on the connecting door were like fingernails on blackboard. Flinching, she forced herself to add, "There *is* something I have to tell you, though." She couldn't let another perfect opportunity to confess go by. That Garrett was nuzzling her neck, obviously feeling very kindly disposed toward her at the moment, gave her that extra boost in the right direction. "I think it's coincidence that I drew stuff that looked like the targets."

"Mmm. That's why we need to run more tests. To be certain."

"Garrett—" She felt her concentration leaching away. "I have to tell you—"

Lightning exploded so close the thunderclap seemed simultaneous. Smedley squawked and thudded the door. As the hail softened into rain, Kate's fingers and toes gradually unclenched, and the dog's yelps subsided into rhythmic hiccups.

Laughing weakly, she caught Garrett's exploring hand. "I'm sorry. I just can't seem to get into the spirit of this."

"Perhaps the situation calls for more drastic, distracting action."

He threw one leg over her knees, roughly poked another button out of its socket, and buried his nose in her neck. The slight stubble of his jaw abraded the hollow of her throat in a pleasantly painful way that ground her mouth shut on a groan. Eager to feel the same scrape against her breast, she shamelessly clutched a handful of his hair to guide his face downward.

The telephone shrilled, alarming them. Garrett's whiskers burned her skin, and Kate pulled his hair.

"Damn!" they said in unison, and Smedley's hics converted to yaps.

Kate heard something rip as Garrett fought to extract his hand to reach for the phone. The water bed, under their efforts to sit up, quaked in counterpoint to the persistent bell and Smedley's relentless lamentations.

Cursing under his breath, Garrett grabbed for the phone and accidentally sent it clanking to the floor. One final splash, and he was off the bed, warning Smedley, as the door trundled open, about dog pounds.

Tracing the telephone down its dangling cord, Kate listened to hollow humming before reassembling it by touch and scrabbling it onto the headboard shelf. She laid a hand to her agitated heart and sighed. Sounds from the kitchen indicated Garrett had taken Smedley there, to reward him with food, no doubt.

As calm returned, Kate realized the telephone had not stopped humming. Worse, when she turned slightly, meaning to adjust it in its cradle, the sound seemed to expand from somewhere to her right, a high, clear, whale-like moan.

"Garrett!"

The mysterious presence harmonized with her squeal.

As she scrambled off the bed, the phone resumed its clamor, helping to push her through the doorway into Garrett's arms.

"There's someone in there," she said, speaking into his shirt front.

9

KITCHEN LIGHT SPILLED across the hall floor, signifying power—if not reason—had been restored. Garrett stretched past Kate to flip the bedroom light switch. The room came into view, all innocence except for the rumpled bedspread.

The telephone continued to bleat. Setting Kate firmly to one side, Garrett strode to snatch it up and yell, "What?" into the receiver. Twisting around, he aimed it at her. "For you."

She hesitated, feeling like a wimp, and he said more kindly, "it's safe in here. The caterwauling is Fred."

The fact that Garrett believed his plant could scream was not the reassurance Kate needed. Furthermore, it wasn't safe to talk on a telephone during a thunderstorm. Stepping just far enough into the room to accept the receiver at arm's length, she raised it gingerly toward her ear.

"Hello," boomed out. "Kate? Kathy the Great? Are you there?"

"How did you get this number?" she asked Bing coldly.

"I told one of the aunts it was an emergency."

"It had better be," she threatened.

"How you coming with our little project?"

"I can't talk about it now!" She glared at Garrett as if he were responsible.

"Oh, I get you. That's not why I called anyway. A little group of us are sitting here enjoying a few drinks, and I bet them fifty bucks I knew an honest-to-God psychic who could read my mind long-distance."

She could hear the liquor on his voice now. "No. I'm hanging up."

"Just one card. Jimmy, you pick it out of the deck."

"No, Captain. Not now." She shoved the receiver at Garrett.

"Shall I slam it home?" he asked.

"Feel free."

Phone put away, hands in jeans pockets, he grinned. "Old boyfriend?"

"A friend and male and old, yes. My psychic powers tell me he will soon meet a hangover."

"I forgot to tell you about Fred." He waved her closer. "I got a new toy for my philodendra. You saw their energy as lines on a graph. This gadget converts the same electromagnetic currents into sound waves." He fiddled with a dial, and Fred's one-note samba grew louder, then softer. "I should have shut it off. Sorry it scared you."

She threw up her hands in a "hey" gesture. Feeling uncharacteristically awkward, she glanced at the phone, the floor, and Garrett's bare feet. She couldn't remember when he'd taken off his shoes and socks. Smedley's toenails clicked across the hall floor behind her.

"Listen, it's been an interesting evening, but I think I better go home and read a book now."

"If you rush off, I'll take it out on the flora and fauna." He raked a frustrated hand through his hair.

She had to smile at his disappointed face. "Could I please have a rain check? I do have a big day delivering balloons tomorrow."

"Heavy lifting, huh?" He stopped her, a hand on her arm, to rebutton her dress; she'd never thought of putting clothes *on* as erotic.

"Thank you for a lovely supper." Politeness was a habit; her mind was definitely elsewhere.

Wrapping his arms around her waist, he said earnestly, "Next time I'll send the dog to sleep over with a friend."

"Yours or his?" She laughed, gripping her own wrists behind his back.

"I'll disconnect Fred. And the phone."

Many miles away, thunder was grating on someone else's nerves. Kate wedged her head under Garrett's chin and yawned contentedly.

"So how about Saturday?" he asked, resting his face in her hair.

"Not Saturday. I have to work all evening." She'd tell him about the magic performance, with its own canine problem, after the fact. When the moment was right.

"Sunday I'm helping friends move across town," Garrett said. "And Monday's too far away. How about tomorrow night? Same time, same station."

"I'd like that." She tilted back to give him one last smile and kiss.

In the hallway Smedley heaved a martyr's sigh.

SHE SHOULD HAVE STAYED and made fierce love with Garrett and then told him about Bing. He would have been so euphoric as a result of all the pleasure she'd given him, he'd have forgiven her and made love again, with even fiercer passion. Twenty minutes after having left his house, she found herself at her own, hoping she hadn't run any red lights.

Corliss and Hank were about to go to bed. As goodnights were exchanged, the phone churred in the kitchen.

"I'll get it."

"I wouldn't be surprised if that's Jamie Bing," Corliss said, her expression slightly pained. "He's been making rather a nuisance of himself tonight. He called again just ten minutes ago, and we *told* him he'd have to cultivate patience."

"Or abstinence," Hank added tartly.

"Sorry, ladies," Kate called behind her. "I've got some sobering news to give him."

Without bothering to turn on the light, she managed to rake a chair away from the table, and, sitting down, lifted the receiver.

"Listen," she snarled. "If you can afford to pay me a thousand bucks, you can afford to lose a fifty-dollar bet."

The open line hissed quietly. Belatedly, she said, "Hello?"

"Uhh, I think I have a wrong number," Garrett said.

Mentally groaning at her stupidity, Kate faked a laugh. "No, I'm the one in the wrong. I'm glad it's you and not who I thought it was."

"Uh-huh." There seemed to be a pause while he tried to remember why he'd phoned. "Tomorrow. We didn't discuss if you were going to be in for more testing. Mr. Garcia wants to see something involving psychokinesis, and as I recall, you did, too."

"I'm sure I'm free in the morning. I have to work in the afternoon. And I have a big date in the evening."

"Ten o'clock," he confirmed, preoccupation thinning his voice. "See you, Kate."

She slapped down the phone, clicked on the light, squinted at the scrap of paper magnetized to the refrigerator door, and dialed the number indicated on it with quick, careless jabs. When the hotel clerk answered, she asked for Bing and drummed fingers on the table, waiting.

I quit, she'd say. *You can write your book about something else. Garrett's incorruptible, his work is impeccable. And don't call me anymore without an appointment, you, you—pimp!*

But, of course, Bing had left a do-not-disturb order at the desk which the switchboard operator refused to violate, even for an "emergency."

"I REALLY DON'T CARE MUCH for psychokinesis," Garrett said. "Testing for it is deadly dull. And I've never seen any successes."

He had just thumped a glass box that resembled a waterless fish tank with an enclosed top, in front of the little group of volunteers. Inside was a pen on a graph, much like the lie detector he'd wired to Fred.

"If you want to try to influence this plotter, I suggest you concentrate on it as a group." Garrett flipped a switch that began the paper spooling from one side of the box to the other, the pen leaving a straight mark across the paper. "See if you can drive the pen higher on the graph just by collective concentration."

Mr. Garcia held up an imperious hand. "I want Perry to examine the box first."

Nicki, who'd come to the session in her usual neon-hued jumpsuit, tipped her chair back, wrapping her ankles around its front legs, prepared to wait. Shrugging at Garrett's wave toward the box, Perry shuffled over to squint at it.

"Sealed on all sides," he said, poking at the top edge with his fingernails. "Including the lid."

"You can't blow on the pen and make it move?" Mr. Garcia suggested. "No wires or anything sticking out anywhere?"

Kate eyed him thoughtfully.

Perry bent forward, hands on knees, and sighted along each wall of the box, shrugged again, and returned to his seat.

"Like I said." Garrett rested one hip on the tabletop and clasped that knee in his hands. His outstretched leg, long and lean, distracted Kate from speculations about Garcia. "Like I said, this won't be the most scintillating experiment you've ever taken part in. Unless, of course, you can actually move the pen."

"Computers are more fun," Nicki grouched. "Ever tried Volition where you try to make the cursor go up or down?"

"What about spoon bending?" Mr. Garcia overrode her. "I've heard a lot of people can do that."

"True, a lot can." Garrett smiled. "But not with their minds. They cheat. Like a magician using sleight of hand."

Keeping her face studiously blank, Kate said, "You've seen it done? The cheating?"

"Young man here about a year ago, claimed he could do stuff like bend keys just by holding them. He actually was pressing them on the table edge surreptitiously. Then he palmed them to hide the curve till the time came in the testing when he was supposed to 'will' them to bend."

"And you caught him out," Mr. Garcia chuckled approvingly. "Not much gets by you, I bet."

"If any of you ever sees where a test could be fiddled, I want to know. One little loophole can scrap hours of research, because even if there wasn't any cheating, skeptics can argue that there might have been."

Studying the nearest wall with more interest than it deserved, Kate wished they'd change the subject.

Nicki, too, seemed tired of it. "Let's go, you guys. Let's see if we can make that sucker jump the track."

After a flurry of rustling into attitudes of comfortable attention, they fixed four pairs of eyes on the barrel of the blue plastic pen.

Softly and distinctly, Garrett said, "I want you to tell yourselves it's okay to succeed here, to exhibit PK. Just relax a moment and then think of the pen as an enemy you want to push away. Think of the point gliding upward on the paper. Your electromagnetic waves can force it to do that, as long as you believe they can."

When he stopped speaking, the last words snagged in Kate's mind—they can, they can, they can. Mr. Garcia's breathing whistled annoyingly in the otherwise silent room. Resisting the powerful urge to look at Garrett, Kate focused her eyes on the unwavering pen. The lab's covert clock trembled one note for the half hour.

Kate's electromagnetic waves seemed to have plans of their own. It was all she could do to hold her eyelids up, let alone control the pen. The need to yawn cramped her jaw muscles. Just as she was despairing of keeping quiet a minute longer, Garrett stood and stretched.

"Had enough?" he asked.

"We failed you again," Mr. Garcia said sadly. "That line stayed flatter than a taxpayer's wallet. Now what?"

"If you'd like, Mac could tell you a bit about OOB—out of body travel—in case any of you want to try that sometime."

"Gare, did you ever consider there might be some unsympathetic minds around here, interfering with the atmosphere?" Nicki stuck out a belligerent chin and glared at everyone except Garrett. "All I know is, I used to do pretty good on remote viewing till this week with this particular group."

"Maybe it's coincidence," he said diplomatically. "We need a lot more time and tests to get any kind of picture. Now, as you know, Mac has done extensive work in separating mind from body. He's managed to send his consciousness long distances unencumbered."

"How do we know he doesn't just say he can do that?" Mr. Garcia spoke up.

"Over the past five years, he's been tested by various scientists in carefully controlled experiments. For instance, Mac would be in an isolation booth under the eye of one man, while another man in a room in a different building would, without looking at it, turn an ESP card—a heart, or a cross, or whatever—faceup on a shelf above his head. The fact that he didn't know the symbol on the card eliminated the possibilities of telepathy and a remote viewing type situation. Mac was able, more than sixty-five percent of the time, to send his consciousness to that room, look at the card, and, returning, report what it was."

Garrett's audience shifted uneasily in their seats.

"Once his cocker spaniel was put in the target room so researchers could watch her reactions during the time Mac's consciousness was supposed to be visiting it. During the test period, she jumped up, wagging her tail, obviously pleased about something, in the otherwise empty room."

"Ten percent of the world's population has had an OOB experience," Nicki informed them. "I'm going to do it, when I'm not so busy."

"It sounds like a kick," Mr. Garcia said. "Only a little hard to believe."

"Actually," Garrett began, hunching his shoulders to wedge his hands into his jeans pockets, "I've seen Mac do it. I was working late in the office upstairs, and felt a draft. And when I looked up, there was this kind of blue glow between me and the dark window, just for a second. Next day he told me he'd been here, and the time coincided with my little adventure. He told me I was tilted back in my chair with my feet on the desk, eating an apple while I read a trade journal. And I was."

Kate shook her head, wanting to believe it since Garrett had said it.

"I'll get him down here if you want to know more." He lifted the glass PK apparatus between both arms.

But everyone had something else to do, including Kate, whose first Up and Away assignment that day was to meet a senior citizens' picnic at City Park. As the group dispersed into the hall, Mr. Garcia touched her arm.

"Perry and I don't see any tricks here, do you?"

"No. Garrett seems to anticipate all the chances of that quite well. Why do you ask?"

"I'm getting old. I'd hate to be making an old fool of myself." He dry-washed one side of his face with a square hand.

"What's your occupation, Mr. Garcia?" she asked his open eye.

"Retired. Got tired and then retired. I had more different jobs than you could shake a stick at," he said, acting out his words with his cane.

Still not sure what he was doing here, Kate followed his slow limp to the parking lot. He enlivened the route with a tale of how he'd once piloted an uncaged gorilla from Kenya to China, presumably long before he was afraid of being foolish.

10

THE SKY WAS INNOCENT of dark clouds when Kate inspected it on her way to Garrett's. No thunderstorm, and, she hoped, no plants and animals to sabotage this night's romance.

But when she knocked on the apartment door, she heard Smedley's anxious woofing, and it was sister Ann who opened it.

"Hi," Kate said optimistically, when Ann didn't step back to let her in. "Can Garrett come out and play?"

The door did swing wider then, letting out the scent of cinnamon rolls and hot tea. Ann smiled with little conviction and pointed in the direction of the kitchen.

With Smedley snuffling rudely at her legs, Kate crossed the living room, saw with relief the dinette table set for only two, and stepped into the kitchen. Garrett was on his hands and knees, one ear to the floor.

"Aha," he said, flattening one hand under the refrigerator to scrape out a rubber ball. He pushed up to his knees, single-handedly whipped open a brown grocery bag, and popped into it ball, water dish, food dish, and five cans of dog food.

"Smedley is going to spend a few days with Ann," he said, standing up to unhook a leash from the pantry door. "Since I'm going to be gone so much this weekend, helping my friends move." He fluttered four rapid winks at Kate.

Smedley backed up and sat on her foot, watching Garrett apprehensively. Kate caught herself on the verge of feeling guilty.

Behind her, Ann said, "You can leave him till Monday morning. It'll save you a trip."

"Good thinking," Garrett said promptly, tossing another can of dog food into the bag. For Kate's benefit, he added, "Ann teaches kindergarten. Monday I'm giving her class a remote viewing test. We do it at least once a year. I'm trying to prove a theory that children are better at it than adults."

"Because they have more imagination and fewer inhibitions," Kate suggested.

"Right. They haven't learned yet that supernatural subjects aren't respectable in polite society." He stalked Smedley with the leash.

"That being the case," Kate said, watching him corner the dog by the refrigerator and win the brief struggle, "don't some of the parents object to the test?"

"We don't publicize it." He scrubbed the dog's ears and jaw before straightening.

"In other words, you don't tell them."

"We don't even tell the children," Ann spoke up defensively. "It's just a guessing game to them, and it certainly doesn't harm anyone. We give it the last day before summer vacation and they forget they even did it."

"And do they do better than adults?"

"The verdict isn't in." Garrett handed Ann the leash. "We don't have enough samples yet." He gathered up the bag of Smedley's personal effects. "Here we are."

Ann led the parade on the way out with the dog trying to anchor himself in the floor, and Garrett gave Kate another wink just before he closed the outside door after them. She wandered around the living room, considering his taste in magazines—*Sports Illustrated, Scientific American*—in art—a photograph of golden aspen trees, a Maurice Sendak print, and furniture—predominantly modern with just a dash of art deco.

Garrett bustled back in, rubbing his hands briskly as if he'd just made a big sale. He walked straight over to Kate, grasped her shoulders, and kissed the bridge of her nose.

"You look great," he said, stepping back an arm's length to look her over again. She was wearing a rose shirtdress this time.

Draping his arm around her shoulder, he strolled toward the kitchen. "Why don't you help me Monday with the kids? Wear your bunny suit, if you want. Hand out paper and pencils and sing instructions for the test."

"No, thanks." She laughed.

"What part don't you like?" He let go of her to agitate a skillet of sizzling hash browns on the stove. "You'd rather wear the sexy slave girl outfit?"

"I'd rather wear jeans. And not sing."

"Fine. I'll pick you up at your house at nine. Do you like onion in your potatoes?"

"IT SEEMS AS IF I'VE KNOWN YOU all my life, and actually it's only been one week," Kate marveled, leaning back in her chair to savor a last sip of wine.

Across the table, Garrett's eyes were getting darker as the room was filling with the shadows of the night. It was peaceful, the only sound a solo classical guitar thrumming on the stereo. He leaned back, too, hooking a casual elbow over the back of his chair.

"Thanks to Ann for bringing you into my life," he said.

"We would have met anyway, because—" Losing her nerve, Kate retreated from the confession she'd been about to make. "Because I can't imagine never knowing you." She rearranged herself, annoyed. "That sounds dumb."

"No, I understand. What some folks call fate. Could be our subconscious selves had already made contact. Perhaps they were on the same electromagnetic wavelength, guiding us toward one another."

Kate set her glass down and left her hand on the table, in case he wanted to touch it. After a moment of quiet, she said, "Why are you looking at me like that?"

"I was trying to see your aunts in you. Something about the chin, maybe, when you tip it up. You said they're your father's sisters?"

Nodding, Kate reached toward the floor beside the table leg and hauled her handbag into her lap. "I have a picture of my folks," she said, fishing out her billfold and splaying it open between the candles.

Garrett leaned over to look, glanced up at her, then back to the wedding photo, and decided, "You're most like your mother. The blond hair and happy eyes. It's a shame they died so young."

Kate tried to swallow the lump in her throat with another sip of wine. "How often do you get to see *your* parents?"

"They run up for a few days every summer. I think you'll like them and vice versa."

The phonograph clicked off and an expectant hush took it's place.

"I disconnected the telephone." Garrett's voice was lazy-soft.

"I'm honored."

"And the philodendra all have little gags on."

She sputtered an incredulous laugh.

Garrett sighed—a lot like Smedley at his most morose. "Now that it appears we are alone and undisturbed, I'm scared to make a move."

She laughed again. "Chaos turns you on, perhaps. Would you like me to take the initiative?"

"Maybe. If it's not too kinky." He folded his arms to wait, anticipation glinting in his eyes.

"Well—" she considered. "How about—"

Standing, she circled to his side of the table and, facing him, hiked up the hem of her dress to bare her thighs before straddling his knees. Resting both elbows on his shoulders, she bent forward to brush his mouth with hers, then nibble it, then kiss it with delicate touches of tongue to his teeth.

She swayed backward and his hands tightened against her waist. "I like the way it starts," he said.

Bending to meet his mouth for a second helping, Kate felt her groin tighten to the feel of his hand sliding inside her bare thigh. As he drew feathery circles increasingly closer to the elastic boundary of her panties, she traced the line of his muscular neck into his shirt collar, and slowly worked free the top button.

Now his other hand caressed her other thigh, stroking up and under her clothes to cup her hip. Kate rocked gently, enjoying the warmth of Garrett's hands and lips, the feel of her breasts rubbing against his chest, the stretching sensation between her legs.

"Mmm," she broke the kiss to say. "You seem to be over your fear."

"But it could return at any moment, so don't rest on your laurels."

She tilted her head, stretching her throat in a soft shout of laughter. "I think I'm resting on yours. Something of yours, anyway."

He buried his nose in her cleavage. "Hussy."

"What?" she feigned outrage.

"I said, 'Hurry.'" His fingers kneading her tingling skin abruptly wrested away, out of her clothes.

"Ohh," she protested. "Don't go."

"I'm going to the bedroom. You can come, too." He scooped her up as he got to his feet, maneuvering her sideways past the table, and bouncing her higher on his chest as he strode purposefully across the room.

Arms around his neck, she grinned with anticipation.

Setting Kate on her feet, Garrett twitched down the bedspread. The room was dim, the only light coming secondhand through the hall door, enough to show his grave face swinging toward her, but not enough to reveal the expression in his eyes. She laid her hand against his cheek. He laid his against her breast.

They blended together—arms, bodies, faces. Between them, Garrett's hand patiently unfastened buttons, his and hers. She was so aroused she couldn't stand any longer. She sank to the edge of the bed, and he coasted with her, still holding the small of her back with one hand and the last button fastening her blouse together.

Her own hands had slid inside his shirt to explore the springy mat of hair across his chest, the rigid nipples, the smooth skin stretched across his ribs. She leaned away so that she could trace her fingertips into his navel, track his stomach into the waistband of his slacks.

His breathing was loud in her ears as she coaxed the single button free and slid the zipper down. With the back of her hand, she gently massaged his waist, and then hooked her fingers under the band of his shorts, drawing them downward.

"Kate," he sighed. "Ahh, Kate."

He felt wonderful in her hand. She wanted desperately to feel him inside her.

"Take these off," she whispered.

When he let go of her to comply, she twisted out of her dress, fighting it off her shoulders and elbows, clumsy with desire. Garrett's strong fingers reached to help with the bra. Stretched full length beside her, marvelously naked, eyes glittering in the dim light, he hauled the remaining undergarments down her legs with a hurried enthusiasm that matched hers.

She rolled against him, wrapping arms and legs around him, kissing his mouth furiously, as if she were drowning and it was oxygen. She felt him laugh before his lips and tongue and teeth returned the kiss, and they rocked together, making the water mattress slap and smack.

Then she felt one of his hands glide across her hip and into the hollow between her thighs. Spreading her legs, he fitted himself between them, tipped her onto her back, and began the slow mating dance that would transport them both to the brink of ecstasy.

Clutching his back, eyes shut to concentrate on the growing sensation, Kate moaned and sighed and laughed and, eventually, screamed.

Garrett, who'd been struggling to hold on to his own passion's eruption, shut his eyes and surrendered to overwhelming sensation. With Kate's sweet scent in his nostrils, her soft, strong legs embracing his hips, her never still hands urging him deeper, he spiraled into release, shivering again and again.

They continued to cling to each other, panting hard, trembling with aftershocks. Garrett rolled sideways, still holding her, so they lay face-to-face. Gradually their grips relaxed, and he raised one slow hand to comb her hair behind her ear.

"I had a very good time," Kate announced gravely.

"You're welcome any time you want to *come* again," he said, trying to keep a straight face.

"You sure you aren't married?" she asked, suddenly distant.

"Not married. And you?"

Kate couldn't believe her luck. She hauled his arm closer to nuzzle the inner part of his elbow. "Nope." Dropping back, she gently stroked his jawline with her fist. "I do have kind of a confession to make, though." Opening her hand, she slid it into the thicket of his hair.

"Confession, huh? Sounds serious. I'll read you your rights first. You have the right to remain bare in my bed, to have any part of me used against you, to—uhh, I forget the rest."

During the recitation, his prowling hand was extremely distracting; Kate shut her eyes on a particularly interesting pinch and tried again to say her piece. "No, Garrett, I have to make a clean breast of it."

Since this was apropos of the current pincering maneuver, they both giggled. Scuffled. Kissed.

Kate's resolve ebbed as her limbs went weak with renewed desire. "Garrett," she breathed.

Something—a gust of breeze or a breath—stirred the top of her hair. Reflexively opening her eyes, she felt more than saw Garrett's head turn to the side. In the darkness, a patch of blue, like the haze of cigarette smoke, hung near the ceiling.

Garrett began to swear, low at first, then with more enthusiasm.

Still befuddled by desire, Kate whispered thickly, "What's wrong?"

He let go of her and struggled to sit up, inexplicably shaking his fist toward the wall. "Get out of here, you damn fool Peeping Tom!" he said.

Kate ripped the top sheet loose and, clutching it to her chest, managed to get out of bed and backed into the closet door with a muffled crash. "Is it—"

"Mac," Garrett growled. "Wait till I get my hands on him."

The blue glow faded into black. Kate marched to the doorway and swiped the wall till she found the switch to turn on the light. They squinted at each other, their postures defensive.

"You mean," she said, horror pinching the words off short, "that was Mac, taking an out of body trip? And that he could just drop in on us any time like that, whether we close the door or not?"

"Now, Kate, I don't think he'd do that now that he knows what we're doing."

Her voice skidded an octave higher. "Are you kidding? Now that he knows what we're doing, he won't be able to keep himself away! He probably went for popcorn and a beer, the better to enjoy the show!"

"Kate—" he began. "Kate!" he shouted as she stooped to grab up a handful of clothes and tried to wrestle them on without lowering the sheet.

Throwing up his hands, he rolled out of bed and jammed his legs into his jeans. "Let's have some coffee or something. The evening's still young."

"I'll see you Monday, Garrett," she said, frantically stuffing buttons into buttonholes. "I'm sorry, I just couldn't—relax again tonight."

"I'll talk to Mac," he promised as she whipped open the outside door. "I'll make him sign a pledge!" he yelled as she slammed it behind her.

Alternating between unreserved joy at having found Garrett and unreserved anger at Mac for giving them something to laugh about some day in the far future, Kate drove home.

11

THE FIRST THING SHE NOTICED when she came through the front door was the telephone being cut off in mid-ring. Following the murmur of Corliss's voice into the kitchen, she composed what she'd say to Garrett, who'd be calling once again to apologize for his intrusive colleague.

It's okay, she'd say. *There are things I'd hate a lot more for him to see me doing than making love.*

But it was Bing. Patting her aunt's shoulder as the receiver changed hands, Kate demanded, "Now what do you want?"

"Your cordiality overwhelms me. What a delight to hear your sweet voice, Kathy."

"Are you sober this time?" She dropped her purse on the table and, tucking the phone under her chin, extracted a clean glass from the dishwasher to fill with tap water.

"I've been asked to stay for another week, held over for an extended engagement in beautiful downtown Las Vegas."

"Because you're that good or because the next scheduled act can't make it?" She put the moist cool glass against her forehead.

"We have a bad connection," Bing said coolly. "You sound like a rusty hinge."

"Why did you call, Captain?" she asked, her voice not so stringent.

"To inquire about your progress with the good Dr. Brody. How many experiments have you managed to sabotage? I hope you're keeping notes."

"Bing, I haven't cashed your five-hundred-dollar check. I'll give it back, next time I see you." He started to splutter, and she overrode it with, "I just can't do any cheating. The tests are too well planned and monitored. I'm not as good a magician as Dr. Brody is a scientist. Even you wouldn't be able to put anything over on him. You better think up some other subject to write your bestseller about. Like how to win bets by pretending to read minds long-distance."

"Didn't you insinuate yourself into his work? Didn't you get hands-on experience?"

"Oh, yeah, I had tactile experience all right." She raised her eyebrows, mirroring Corliss's expression as the older woman folded laundry across the table.

Bing scolded and pleaded like a coach at halftime. When he paused to draw a breath, Kate threw the rest of her bombshell. "I'm beginning to think there's something to this ESP stuff after all. And tonight I had an experience that I'd swear involved an out of body traveler."

There was some heavy wheezing on the other end of the line while Bing absorbed all this.

"Maybe you'd like to visit Garrett's lab when you get back home. See for yourself," she suggested.

He continued to hyperventilate.

"Listen," she said cheerfully. "I've got this cute new trick—materializing a puppy. Or a gerbil or whatever. Hank made me a box—"

"I thought you had more sense than that!" he shouted into her ear.

"It's no big deal," she began, confused. "You can kind of hold their mouths shut so they can't—"

"You've got a crush on him. He's tall, dark, and handsome, and you let him get to you!"

"Well, yeah, you could describe it that—"

He hung up on her. Thoughtfully cradling her own telephone, Kate tipped her glass of water into the sink.

"Out of body?" Corliss said, smartly snapping a pillowcase before folding it into thirds.

"It was like your bingo fire without the bingo or the fire. Just smoke and a breeze that ruined the festivities." Stretching, smiling, Kate started heading for her bedroom.

"Out of one's body would be such a refreshing change," Corliss said dreamily. "So often it's the mind that's out."

SATURDAY WAS ONE OF Colorado's finest. Not too cool, not too warm, not too cloudy, not too breezy. It was the kind of day that wouldn't be "too" anything except short.

Kate, in white painter's pants and an orange Bronco T-shirt, crouched in the flower beds behind the house, clearing out the deadwood. Through the open kitchen window overhead, she could hear breakfast dishes being loaded into the washer and a mild argument about whether a mayonnaise facial was appropriate material for the cookbook.

Corliss—the yea vote—was saying, "Cooking without a license doesn't imply eating without one."

Hank—the nay vote—yielded with, "Well, if someone should make the mistake of eating it, that would certainly be a new wrinkle."

Appreciative laughter for the pun had to be shushed. "There's the door."

Moments later, a male voice approaching the kitchen prickled Kate's arms with gooseflesh. Garrett.

"Kate! You have a visitor," Hank shouted.

"Coming!" Kate called, stripping off her work gloves and leaping for the backdoor.

He looked terrific, tall and tanned, hair damp with heat, lounging in the hall doorway as if this was his home. Kate wanted to grab and kiss the living daylights out of him.

"Good morning," she said serenely, lifting her own hot hair off the nape of her neck. "What's up?"

He raised his hand and waved her billfold at her. "You left this on the table last night."

"Oh my gosh, I hadn't even missed it yet," Kate gasped, her jubilant mood deserting her.

"What if a policeman had stopped you?" Corliss scolded. "Or you ran out of gas?"

But it wasn't missing her precious license or credit cards that upset Kate; it was whether Garrett had seen her other ID, including her membership in the Association of Professional Magicians of America.

She stared into his eyes as the wallet changed hands. He stared back blandly.

"You can count the money; it's all there," he suggested unhelpfully.

"You're just the man we wanted to see," Corliss said, reaching past Kate to draw him to the table. "Sit down and taste these."

"These," were six heaping platters of cookies.

"Would you rather have milk or coffee?" Corliss continued to herd Garrett toward the taste test. "Each batch was made with a different kind of flour, and we want to know which you like best."

Obediently, Garrett sat, tucking the napkin Hank handed him into his open collar, hefting the first golden cookie and taking one fearless bite.

Corliss sat opposite him with her spiral notebook at the ready to jot down his reaction. Hank poured him a scalding cup of coffee that was giving off enough heat waves to cause mirages. Kate sank into the rocking chair, still waiting for a sign that her cover had been blown.

"Mmm. Mmmhmm," Garrett judged, chewing hard, showing off his facial muscles.

"That one's graham flour. Should I tell him that or not, Hank?"

"I think he ought to have a sip of water before he tries the next one," Hank said. "To clean his palate."

"Shouldn't he be spitting each bite out instead of swallowing it?"

"Ladies, I couldn't force myself to do that," Garrett protested gallantly. "These are too good." He picked one off the next plate.

"That batch was the corn flour, wasn't it, Hank?" Corliss confirmed it herself by eating one.

"Unusual," Garrett mumbled, losing a few taste buds on a slurp of scorching coffee.

The tasting continued. Corliss carefully recorded Garrett's every comment, then tried each of the cookies in question to see if she agreed. Hank, observing at first by hovering over his shoulder, gravitated toward a chair and began absently munching cookies at random, throwing in such pertinent remarks as, "This one tastes like shoe polish," and "We should have baked Alka-Seltzer into this one." The session deteriorated from a carefully controlled test to a casual scarfing down of everything in sight.

Meanwhile, Kate gently rocked, worry niggling at her. If she'd told him all about herself when she'd had the chance, she wouldn't be sitting here hoping his good sportsmanship would stretch as far as magicians who play dirty tricks.

"Garrett, would you let Corliss and me test for mental telepathy at your lab sometime?" Hank resumed chewing very slowly.

He belched politely into his fist. "I'd be delighted. I've never had a chance to experiment with twins. Have you had psychic experiences, either or both of you?"

"A few, now and then," they said in unison.

Garrett turned around and winked at Kate. The dazzling smile accompanying it made her head swim with relief; feeling reprieved, she grinned back. He left soon afterward, declining in a voice tinged with hysteria, the aunts' invitation to stay awhile and have lunch.

Several times during the day, Kate reflected on her good fortune—that Garrett had not snooped, that she could still tell him her secret at the right time and in the right place. She promised herself she really would.

THE PERFECT DAY FADED into a perfect evening, and Kate drove to the birthday party with her magic box.

Kevin Rathburn was the guest of honor—turning five. Eight boys and five girls of similar size and exuberance helped him welcome Kate into the crepe-papered and ballooned family room. Others present were parents Rathburn, grandmother Rathburn, baby sister Rathburn—and—just the person Kate was looking for—older brother Rathburn. She excused herself and him into the laundry room to explain the trick.

"I need you help, Barry," she said, after establishing that was his name.

He shrugged hard and sniffed harder. His sober expression might have indicated either shyness or distaste for being trapped in the house with a bunch of preschoolers. It was probably a result of the latter. He looked about eight years of age.

Squatting beside him conspiratorially, Kate repinned the silk orchid behind her left ear and picked lint from her long purple skirt. "I need an assistant for this trick, see, and you look like my man. Okay?"

He shrugged again. There was a crash in the distance as if, at the least, one wall had caved in.

Pulling forward the bunny box, Kate said, "Magicians don't ever tell outsiders how they do their tricks. You willing to give your sacred promise not to reveal to anyone—*anyone*—how we pull the dog out of thin air?"

She'd finally fanned a spark. His eyes narrowed and focused as he nodded. "Cross my heart," he said in a surprisingly deep voice.

It became obvious he hadn't known about the puppy, which might have explained his sudden interest in what Kate was proposing to do. He volunteered to get the animal from a parent, smuggle it into the laundry room, and practice the illusion with Kate. She leaned on the dryer and studied a shelf of detergents till he came back with a bath towel draped over his arms.

The pudgy black Labrador underneath was gently snoring. His silky sides rose and fell in blissful ignorance. When they transferred him carefully into the secret compartment, he fit it with enough space on all sides.

Completely motivated now, Barry grinned at the dog, at Kate, at his own reflection in the wall mirror. He listened, scratching his nose, while she explained how she wanted him to bring her the box, the open lid concealing the puppy behind.

Their star suddenly wakened, yawned with his whole face, and craned his neck trying to see where he was. Still, he let himself be arranged and rearranged in repeated practice of the trick till Kate was satisfied and Barry was fairly dancing with anticipation.

"Can you keep him quiet and out of sight till I'm ready for him?" Kate asked, eyeing the increasingly active dog with doubt.

"I'll take him out in the garage and play with him," Barry offered unselfishly.

"Good. If he's tired, it'll be easier to put him through the box. I'll need him in about twenty minutes, so you be back with him by then."

He was wearing a watch which they solemnly synchronized with hers.

The sergeant at arms seemed to be Grandma Rathburn; she organized the party into an audience sitting cross-legged on the carpet four feet from Kate's tripod table. While the children settled down, Kate surveyed the room for mirrors and other shiny surfaces that might reflect some of her secrets. Repositioning the velvet-draped table three feet farther from the fidgeting feet of a front row spectator, she whipped a huge bouquet of spring flowers out from under her armpit.

"Ohh! Ahh!" the children shouted.

"She had it up her sleeve," a voice piped up.

Ignoring it, Kate picked up a little orange bucket from the table and flashed its empty bottom at the children. "My name is Kate," she enunciated without raising her voice. "And sometimes I need you to say the magic words for magic to happen. Today's magic words are—"

She held the bucket in one hand, by the lip, and pretended to be thinking, staring at the ceiling, the floor, and frowning. The other hand was casually jammed into her lavender jacket pocket.

"Rice Krispies!" she said, pretending she'd just remembered, as she yanked her hand out, forefinger pointing up, two coins palmed out of view. "Let's see if you can say it altogether. Ri-i-ice Krispies!"

As the chorus crescendoed, Kate snapped her fingers, and a coin popped up between them. To gratifying giggles, she continued to grab money out of the air and rattle it into the bucket. She moved into the audience to pull coins from ears, hair, knees, and elbows, concentrating on the birthday boy. Shaking the bucket and running a fistful of coins through her fingers, she waggled her eyebrows in a manner reminiscent of Harpo Marx and burrowed under Kevin's collar to bring out a two dollar bill that she held high for all to admire before presenting it to him.

"It was up her sleeve," came the same, slightly nasal voice that had tried to expose her earlier.

Depositing the bucket on the floor so she could roll up her sleeves, she turned around and spotted him in the little crowd. He both sounded and looked like a miniature Andy Rooney. Showing him and the others her arms bared to the elbows, encouraging them to intone the magic words, Kate threw a mock right hook at the pint-size heckler's chin and materialized a coin on the follow-through.

He grinned and opened his mouth to comment.

"How many of you can count to ten?" she rushed to inquire. "Let's hear you. One, two—" She widened her eyes, impressed, while they shouted numbers and she set up the next trick.

The act went smoothly, the children participating with enthusiasm. She kept her sleeves pushed well up, sweater style, during the linking rings, sponge balls, torn paper and rope tricks. Her heckler tried to spoil the show a couple times. "It's in her pocket," he'd announced, but he subsided under his peers' protests. "Shut up, Oscar," they shouted. Kate wasn't surprised he was a troublemaker, with that name to live down.

"I need you to say the magic words one more time. Not yet!" she hastened to add as a straggling, halfhearted chorus of "Rice Krispies" began.

Brushing her sleeves down to her wrists, sure that Oscar would never believe a puppy came out of them, she twisted to check on Barry's whereabouts. He lurked on the other side of the doorway by the kitchen, and brought one hand into view, waving it weakly.

"Mr. Barry Rathburn is going to assist me with this illusion," Kate announced. Kevin and friends catcalled and booed. "Let me just check to see if he is ready."

She'd left the box on a chair just inside the kitchen. Out of sight of the audience, she and Barry loaded it with the puppy whose whiskers now sported cobwebs and black coat glittered with sawdust. Barry had obviously given him a thorough workout.

Kate returned briskly to her table. "Now when I count to three, you say the magic words very softly. Very softly. Barry?"

Walking slowly and stiffly, as if he were carrying full coffee cups, Barry brought Kate the box. She took it, thanking him with a big smile, using one forefinger to keep the lid propped up between the audience and the puppy-filled secret compartment. She glanced down into one bright, beady black eye before showing the box's interior all around.

"One," she said, resting the box on her stomach, shutting the lid, and swinging the compartment inside. There was one quiet yip of protest.

"Twooo," she said, offering all sides of the closed box for her viewers' perusal.

"And softly, now. Three."

"Rice Krispies!" they breathed obediently as she lifted the lid and scooped one hand under the mound of fur.

In that brief period of time, the pup had fallen into exhausted sleep. When she scooped him out, he lolled limply on her palm. The children hadn't yet decided what she was holding when Barry, at her elbow, blurted out with horror, "Did we kill him?"

"Eee!" the nearest tiny female mourned. Then the party surged forward, eager to decide for themselves if this handful of fluff was, *A*. real, and *B*. dead.

Kate vaguely heard herself shout for quiet, her exhortations only adding to the din. The pup, meanwhile, was startled into awakening. His resurrection touched off an equally noisy cheer. Quivering like Don Knotts, the Labrador widened an apologetic eye a moment before Kate felt the warm liquid running up her arm.

12

"SO THERE I AM with my sleeve a sponge, soaking up Pup's accident," Kate was telling her giggling aunts at lunch the next day. "And Oscar is so delighted with the irony of it. He's jumping up and down yelling, 'It's in her sleeve, in her sleeve!'"

"But the pup's all right?" Hank said, wiping her eyes with her napkin.

"Oh, yeah." Kate stood to fetch the coffeepot. "He was fine once we took him to a quiet room." She stored half a ham sandwich between her lips to free her hands for pouring.

"We ought to get another dog, Corliss."

"I thought we agreed no more dogs after that last one—Tuffy."

"Tuffy was a Dandie Dinmont," Hank enlightened Kate. "That's a short-legged English terrier, but we called him a dandy dimwit, because he'd go off in a trance every now and then. His eyes would glaze over and he'd wander around like a zombie till someone rattled the dog food sack, and then he'd miraculously snap right out of it."

Corliss threw back her head, cascading mirth. "Tuffy got spacier and spacier and fatter and fatter—"

"Cats are nicer," Kate said, thinking of Smedley.

GARRETT CALLED HER Sunday evening—just to reconfirm Monday morning's engagement, he said.

"Don't use the word 'engagement' to an old maid," Kate teased. "Unless you like being trampled."

"I'm not sure. Is that like when a female crushes her body against mine and—"

"I don't think the phone company tolerates this kind of talk on their lines."

"I can't stand much more of it myself."

She gave him a predictable snicker. "Did you finish moving your friends already?"

"No, they're giving me a ten minute break."

"Nice folks to work for."

In the background a feminine voice screeched and exploded into extravagant laughter. Garrett chuckled some aside, and Kate grimaced with a twinge of jealousy, feeling she'd lost his attention.

"Well," he said—at that moment she could picture his broad back straightening, his long fingers tightening on the receiver, ready to break their connection. "Jen is putting the leg irons on again. I'll pick you up about nine in the morning."

"Honk if you love noise," she said, wanting to have the last word.

GARRETT DIDN'T HAVE TO SOUND the horn the next morning. Kate was waiting on the front porch swing and hopped up to wait at the curb as soon as she saw him coming.

"Gonna be a hot day," Garrett said as she bounced into the front seat. "Nice dress."

"Supposed to be the hottest so far. Nice shirt," Kate said, returning the compliment.

He used a neighbor's driveway for a turnaround, and gave Kate's knee a friendly squeeze as they set out down the narrow street.

"Where's Mac?" she asked, not really caring.

"He's coming separately."

"Sounds painful."

Concentrating on traffic, Garrett was quiet till they reached the city limits.

"Did you do anything exciting yesterday?" He glanced sideways long enough to notice a strand of hair over her eye. Brushing it back, his hand, lingered against her cheek, sending a ripple of pleasure down her spine.

"Nothing. The highlight was talking to you on the phone." Just before he withdrew his hand, she turned to kiss it.

"That dull, huh?"

"You weren't sick Saturday, were you?" She grinned at the memory of Garrett and her aunts, eyes glazed, discussing wheat versus rye, over six almost empty plates.

"No, but I never want to see another cookie till at least August."

"You certainly won them over. I bet they dedicate the book to you."

"They won me over, too. Corliss is the one who has a passel of children?"

They were skimming along Highway 93 now, the foothills and flatirons to their left, the flat expanse of eastern plains to their right.

"Eight children and ten grandchildren, and not one lives closer than three hundred miles. She gripes about not seeing them until one family or another swarms in for a visit, and then she's grateful for the peace of long-distance phone calls."

"Her husband's been dead quite a while?"

"About thirteen years. Mr. Trilby, as she still refers to him, was in the U.S. diplomatic service. He died of an African fever, of all things in this day and age." She frowned at the chain and barbed wire fence dividing Rocky Flats and its nuclear power facilities from the rest of the dry, tan landscape.

"And Hank never married? Some poor guy doesn't know what he's missed."

"Hank seems to have been perfectly happy that way. When she and Corliss were twenty, my father was born—big surprise to everyone. At the same time, Corliss was pregnant with her first child. She and her mother both had morning sickness something awful, and difficult births. Hank said that if that was what having a man did for you, she'd pass. At least that's the way she tells it now."

The car crested a rise and, miles in the distance, Boulder glittered as it nestled in its valley.

"So which aunt do you most resemble?" Garrett wondered.

"I hope I'm the best of each—independent and capable like Hank, generous and maternal like Corliss."

He turned his head from the beautiful view and considered her as if she were the scenic attraction. Nervously, she gestured toward the windshield.

Eyes facing in front of him again, Garrett squirmed into a straighter position. "What did you do the rest of Saturday?" he asked. "You had to work?"

Here it was. Another golden opportunity to tell him about the magic side of her life.

"Saturday night I had a preschooler's birthday party," she began reluctantly.

"Now that, I bet, was not boring."

He adjusted the rearview mirror and the air conditioner, braked for and passed a farm tractor, reached to switch on the radio, turning to a news station. Minutes were seeping by and Kate couldn't seem to find the perfect opening line to her confession. While the news distracted him, Kate admired Garrett's strong hands on the wheel and imagined them gripping various parts of her anatomy instead.

She'd wait. She'd tell him when she could have his full attention, when she could soften the news with well-placed kisses and other inducements.

ANN'S KINDERGARTEN CLASS fidgeted and tittered through her introduction of the three people who would be playing a guessing game with them. Having given Garrett their rapt attention as he explained the rules, they thundered, "Goodbye, Mac," to send him on his way to the target. Then the class roiled outside for recess, leaving Kate and Garrett alone in the sun-streaked, lilliputian-furnished room.

Garrett strolled along the backboard, hands clasped behind his back, like an art critic examining the lineup of overhead crayoned drawings. Kate sat on Ann's desk, legs dangling, and admired the way his dark hair swirled against the collar of his dress shirt, the way his jeans rode his hips and molded his narrow rear end.

She sure hoped she could get him alone again soon, someplace where Mac couldn't find them.

As if Garrett could, indeed, see what she was thinking, he said, leaning closer to examine what was either a dragon or a green horse, "I made Mac promise to telephone first the next time he decides to pay me a visit."

"That really was him, huh?" It suddenly occurred to her that even if she wanted to complain about the experience to some bosom buddy, she'd get derision instead of sympathy.

"Mmm. So, Ms. Christopher, what are you doing every night this week?"

She shifted her weight on the desk top. "It's not very polite to make me admit I don't have a date every night."

"Now you do." He turned and, above his smile, his eyes were full of subliminal messages.

As the room went still, the playground babble swelled, and beyond that, the nasal hoot of a train could be heard. A shadow rolled across the floor, darkening Garrett's skin, as a scudding cloud intercepted the sun. Kate felt the edge of the desk cutting into her thighs, felt the weight of her free-swinging feet, but especially felt the swoop of pleasure through her pelvis as he continued to eye her with desire.

"Have I told you what a lovely woman you are?"

She'd always had trouble accepting this kind of dramatic compliment. From Garrett it sounded so honest and fresh, she didn't blush or wisecrack, just shook her head gravely.

"Have I told you you have a personality to match?" He took a step closer and the sun burst free, bathing him in light. "You're magical."

"No, Garrett, truly I'm not," she started to deny. "Well, I *am*, but—"

A police whistle shrilled. Ann's faint but imperious order followed. "Time to go in, class."

Garrett grinned ruefully. "You've made me feel like a teenager again. We've known each other what—a week? And already I'm a sucker under your spell."

"Don't say that!" she cried, pushing off the desk. The subdued clatter of the returning children made her rush and slur the words. "I haven't tricked you in any way!"

Obviously puzzled by her unexpected reaction, Garrett opened and closed his mouth before he turned toward Ann and her tribe, streaming through the doorway.

As the thump and scrape of little feet and furniture died down, Ann announced, "Mrs. Frick's class is going to join us for this game, so if you'll all scoot your chairs closer together to make room, they're coming in right now." To Garrett she said sotto voce, "I assume that's fine with you."

"Oh, sure, the more the merrier. Kate, you want to start handing out the paper and pencils?"

Mrs. Frick, a tiny blonde whose eyebrows seemed stuck in a perpetually pained slant, joined Ann in shushing the children so that Garrett could repeat his instructions. As he finished and asked if there were any questions, a high, familiar voice made Kate turn around abruptly.

"I know her," Oscar said. "She was at Kevin's." Kate started, crumpling paper to her chest. "She pulled a puppy out of a box," the relentlessly triumphant voice continued.

Garrett glanced behind himself, looking for newcomers. "Who're you talking about?" he asked, politely conversational, an indulgent smile tipping the corners of his mouth.

Feeling like a driver skidding toward an inevitable collision, Kate handed one bewildered boy three pencils and no paper.

"Her!" Oscar stood up and pointed. Everyone else swiveled to look at the accused.

"Oh, of course," Garrett said. "Kate. She sings and hands out balloons at parties. Right?" He glanced at his watch, already thinking about something more pertinent.

"No!" Oscar shouted scornfully, making Kate's fixed smile crumble at the edges. "She does neat stuff like grabbing money out of the air, and getting dead dogs out of boxes."

Even Mrs. Frick, who'd been holding her finger to her lips and glaring at Oscar, gave him flat-out attention now.

Garrett glanced blankly toward Kate. "Dead dogs?"

"Not really dead. We thought it was though." Oscar's uninhibited laugh infected everyone but Garrett and Kate.

Gazing at her like he'd seen a ghost, Garrett asked the boy, "A dog out of a box? Like a rabbit out of a hat?"

"Yeah," came the effervescent answer. "She's pretty good for a girl."

The last was emphasized sarcastically, which immediately divided the room into male and female factions, trying to shout each other down, while the two teachers waded forward to restore order.

Even with misery clouding her vision, Kate had no trouble reading Garrett's disbelieving lips. "Magician?"

THE REMOTE VIEWING "game" seemed interminable. Kate hugged herself in a too small, hard plastic chair in the back of the room while Garrett patrolled the front, conspicuously ignoring her. When time was up and she had gathered together all the drawings, he whisked them from her as if she were leprous. They said their goodbyes to Ann and followed Mrs. Frick's skipping, jigging, hopping class into the hall.

"We have to pick up Smedley at Ann's," Garrett said above the top of Kate's head as she paused to let a trio of little girls giggle past her.

She nodded, careful not to lean backward because she might touch him and feel him jerk away. Her mind swarming with explanations, she was learning the meaning of cold sweat. He had to listen. Be understanding. Forgive.

They skirted the last of the children and pushed free into the parking lot. Why hadn't she told him days ago, she mourned, following his ramrod back. Heat radiated from the concrete, branding the soles of her shoes. Even the car seat had the same effect on the back of her legs.

She waited till they'd pulled out of the lot and found a slot in the traffic flow. "Garrett, I have to explain."

"No, you don't." He squinted into the left side mirror and changed lanes.

"Of course I do. You think I didn't tell you I was a magician because I was trying to put something over on you."

"It did cross my mind." His jaw flexed, shutting in whatever else he'd been about to say.

"I was afraid you wouldn't want to be—friends—anymore if you knew my occupation. I did try to tell you, several times, but something always seemed to interrupt."

His one bitter chuckle reminded her of what else the interruption had forestalled. "Magic requires a lot of talent and hard work," he observed coldly. "You shouldn't be ashamed of it."

"You know why I didn't tell you!" She twisted impatiently toward him. "Magicians and parapsychologists are natural enemies. If I'd come bopping up to the lab in my tuxedo and top hat, you'd have thrown me out on my tails."

In spite of himself, Garrett's mouth hovered near a smile for all of two seconds. "So you're perfectly innocent," he said. "Your solitary reason for coming to CROPS was to test your psychic potential."

Kate swallowed hard. A bus commandeering their lane required all of Garrett's attention, thereby giving her a moment's respite. When traffic thinned again, he swung a stern look at her.

"I don't think I'm psychic, no," she admitted. "The reason for my coming to you was—couldn't we talk about this at Ann's? When I can really explain it?"

Garrett shrugged indifferently. He settled closer to his window, away from her.

They wound into a narrow street where all the houses were variations on the same prefabricated theme. A pair of shirtless young men tossing a football sidled reluctantly out of the street just before Garrett made a hard right turn into a driveway lined with marigolds. The house was a moss-colored clapboard tri-level and a mirror image of the beige one next door.

Jerking free of his seat belt, Garrett muttered, "Bing."

"What?" Her heart slipped one notch lower.

"Bing!" He looked squarely at her then, a mixture of pain and anger stoking the fire in his eyes. "You called your drunken friend on the phone 'Captain.' Captain Bing, it has to be. The great illusionist and debunker of all things supernatural."

"Yes, but, Garrett—"

"You work for him. He sent you."

"Yes! But, Garrett—"

"Wait here," he snarled and abruptly got out of the car.

He stalked up the sidewalk to Ann's front door and used a key to open it. Then he disappeared inside.

13

KATE VICED HER HEAD between her hands. Sounds of a ball being kicked, running feet, shouts of laughter filtered through the fingers covering her ears. In a moment, Garrett stepped out again with Smedley capering ecstatically around his feet.

Letting the dog into the back of the car, ordering him sternly and ineffectually to sit, Garrett's eyes skidded away from any contact with Kate's. He slid behind the wheel and slammed the door harder than usual, or necessary.

"I didn't trick you," she rushed to say. "I admit that was the plan, but after I saw you and the careful way you run the lab—"

"You couldn't cheat," he finished for her, wrenching the key to start the car. "I'm too good for you."

"Yes. And I didn't want to cheat anymore. I was dumb to agree to do it in the first place, but Bing—" She leaned an elbow on the back of the seat and shaded her eyes with that hand. "I decided to give him his money back after I got to know you better."

Garrett nodded and nodded, his mouth a grim line. "Do you know," he began with quiet menace, "how much damage you might have done to my credibility? Just knowing that a magician was secretly taking part in my tests, just that could make the tests totally useless as far as my colleagues are concerned." As his master's voice rose, Smedley began whimpering sympathetically. "People like you have no concept of the hours of hard work that might have to be scrapped. You don't care, do you? It's all just a romp to you."

"No! It wasn't. You showed me—"

"I liked you. A lot more than liked. I thought we might have something special going."

"Garrett," she exclaimed, trying to stave off whatever terrible sentence he was about to impose. "Let's start over. Give me a chance to show you how much I respect what you're doing."

"Respect should be mutual," he said tiredly, and she felt the noose settle around her neck. "And I just can't reciprocate."

"I'm sorry." She wiped under one eye with a knuckle, feeling the hollow hopelessness of someone bereaved. "For both of us."

Garrett jabbed the radio on, and offensively loud rock flogged them back to Denver.

THUD, THUD, THUD, thud, thud, she dreamed, and then she awoke in bed. The knocking replayed in her head, so real she held her breath, anticipating another round. When it didn't come, she thrashed free of the sweaty sheet and spread-eagled herself to the night air's chilly caress.

Opportunity, she thought. Thumbing its nose at me. She remembered Garrett's tensed jaw as he braked in front of her house. And heard again his curt, "Goodbye, Kate."

"I guess tonight's off, huh?" she'd asked as lightly as her aching throat would allow.

"*Everything's* off." He stared stoically through the windshield.

She latched the door gently. "Call me sometime?"

"No," he said and drove out from under her hand on the roof.

So stubborn. So dumb. So desirable.

She flounced over onto her stomach and coolness prickled her back. *Right now*—she elbowed up enough to see the clock radio—1:07 in the morning—*I could be stretched out naked next to him, both of us mellow from lovemaking, beginning to think about doing it again.*

Punching her pillow, she jammed her face into it. *I hope you're awake, Garrett Brody. I hope you're kicking yourself for what you're missing, too.*

MILES AWAY, Garrett was lying sleepless in his big, lonely bed. Ever since his last glimpse of Kate slump-shouldered by her curb, he'd wanted to throw something, kick something, hit something. The pent-up anger had finally smoldered out, leaving only this dull ache of betrayal that tortured him into a state of insomnia.

Kate.

He had let her into his life too trustingly. It was going to take a long time to pluck out every trace of her from his mind and heart.

CORLISS, KATHY THE GREAT'S unofficial manager, scheduled several magic shows that week—three birthday parties and one wedding anniversary. Since Doretta was due for a vacation, Kate volunteered to man the switchboard at Up and Away, in addition to delivering and singing after office hours. At home, she was a whirling dervish with cleaning supplies, emptying whole rooms of furniture in an old-fashioned, therapeutic orgy of purification.

In her free time she perfected two new tricks, typed fifty pages of her aunts' manuscript, painted the back fence, and balanced the checkbook she hadn't reconciled for the last eight months.

But though she pelted through the gauntlet of days without looking right or left or—especially—behind, she couldn't escape him. *Garrett.* He was like a song running monotonously through her mind—a nagging splinter in her skin—a bittersweet memory.

Another week began. Jamie Bing flew in from Las Vegas, bringing back his assistant and a grudge against Kate. Pretending not to notice his glowering, gruff attitude, Kate loitered in the magic shop one morning, visiting with Minda.

"How many summer classes are you taking?" Kate asked, practicing palming a card from an open deck by the cash register. It snapped away and spiraled to the floor. "Dang."

"Your hands are too small. A biology and a math."

"How was Vegas? Win anything?"

"*I* could have won fifty dollars," Bing interjected. He was wearing a rumpled white dress shirt and very shiny black trousers, and he needed a haircut.

"I broke even on blackjack. That was the *good* news," Minda said, taking the deck in her own small hands and fanning it. Compared with Bing's, her outfit—designer jeans and a T-shirt—was downright chic.

"Min, why don't you go get yourself a cola and one for me, too?" Bing suggested. He was window-shopping from the inside, arms folded, studying the trickle of pedestrian traffic. "You want something?" he ungraciously added to Kate.

"Nope," she said, choosing a card.

"Me neither." Minda deftly performed a little-finger break below the selected card so she could side-steal and pocket it.

"Sure you do. Here's three bucks," he said, waving the bills.

The women exchanged amused, amazed looks. *Bing was actually buying?*

Minda raked the card into the deck with its mates and stretched, snatching the money just before dropping her arms again. "How long do you want me to be gone?" she asked too sweetly.

"However long it takes!"

Bing's sense of humor, never in plentiful supply, was running on empty. Kate was glad she'd returned the loaded dice and destroyed the IOU two afternoons before he came home to yell at her.

The street door jingled Minda out, and Kate put the cards in their box. "I take it you want to blaspheme me in private."

Bing, who knew dozens of tricks with cigarettes but didn't know how to stop smoking them, swatted himself, searching for a light. "First you can give me my five hundred back. I can't tell you how disappointed I am in you."

She hadn't cashed his check. Playing sleight of hand, she showed it to him, folded it into tenths, changed it into a one dollar bill, tore that into confetti, restored the bill to its original structural integrity then changed it into the check again, and tucked it into his shirt pocket. He tapped a yawn with the back of a fist, putting her in her place as he pretended to be bored.

Sucking nicotine into his lungs, he said, "I've got another job for you. Pays just as good, maybe better."

"Oh? You're giving me one more chance?"

"Terry Lawton is in Reno, Ricky Vigil is in Dallas, that leaves you."

"You silver-tongued master of tact." Waving smoke away from her nose, Kate circled the counter to appropriate Minda's stool. "So what skulduggery does this job involve?"

"Here." Bing snapped a piece off the end of the adding machine tape to write on. "Customer's name and phone number. I'd rather you discuss it directly with him. If it works out, you can pay me a finder's fee."

Kate peered suspiciously at the name "Harvey Smith" and the number, then at Bing's unreassuring smile. "Why does the image of a staked goat suddenly come to mind? What's wrong with this assignment?"

Sighing out a column of smoke irritably, he said, "Madam, I assure you, you should be delighted."

"That's what you thought I'd be the last time."

"Yes, well, I believe this is a lot like that last time." A real smile flipped on and off. His temper was improving as much as hers was deteriorating. "I didn't get the entire gist of it, but Mr. Smith seems to want you to spy on Garrett Brody's lab."

Kate's feet hit the floor and her elbow hit, painfully, the countertop. "He what?"

Chuckling, Bing ground out the cigarette and went to help Minda, who was bumping through the door with three cups in her hands. Kate had torn the paper with the name and address into four before she stopped to think and jammed the scraps into her white shorts pocket.

"Thanks," she told Minda, accepting a cup. "Call Dallas or Reno," she told Bing, making her exit.

UNMINDFUL OF GRASS STAINS, Kate sat on the lawn in City Park and watched a flock of grazing geese, as her mind was busy working out the problem of Harvey Smith and his interest in CROPS. Another would-be author? No. Bing would never have helped a competitor locate a magician.

Why, then, did Smith want to infiltrate Garrett's lab? Kate's imagination unleashed CIA and KGB agents flitting among boulders and trees, clanking with binoculars, walkie-talkies, and guns, documenting Garrett's every move as he approached a breakthrough that would change the world's view of the paranormal.

One sleek black and gray goose drew himself up and hooted.

Okay, too outlandish. Maybe Garrett had a rival in the paranormal business who wanted to steal industrial secrets, as it were.

Naw. She didn't need a goose to remind her that scientists promiscuously share their experiments with anyone interested in duplicating and reconfirming results. Mr. Smith wouldn't need to hire a spy. All he had to do was buy a photocopier.

A white dog—who looked like an improved version of Smedley—cantered enthusiastically after the Frisbee his human friend spun to him. The two crossed from left to right in front of Kate, ignoring the geese.

Kate stretched backward to retrieve the pieces of Bing's printing from her pocket. She reassembled them for the phone number, memorized it, stood up and brushed off her seat. How could it hurt to call Smith and ask about the job? Picturing herself in a beige trench coat, offering herself as a double agent to an effusively grateful Garrett, she jogged toward the car.

SHE DIDN'T EVEN WAIT to get home. Finding a public phone outside the Natural History Museum, she jammed it full of nickles and listened to the rhythmic blips.

"Hello?" a deep, mildly interested voice answered.

"May I speak to Harvey Smith?"

"This is he."

An educated man. She watched a spider skim the concrete past her toes. "This is Kate Christopher. Jamie Bing gave me your name. He tells me you need the services of a professional magician."

"Yes?"

Educated, but maybe not too swift. A passing party of four teenage girls, shrieking joyously, held up Kate's next words, thereby giving Smith some time to think.

"Are you a magician?" he asked.

"Right. Could you tell me about the job?"

"You need to come to the house."

"Couldn't you just tell me on the phone? I'm not sure I really want to apply." Her voice rose defensively as the girls came zigzagging back.

"No," Smith said firmly, brooking no argument. "If you're interested, I'll give you the address."

Having neither paper nor pencil, Kate memorized it, glaring at the girls who'd rolled to a stop a few feet away to debate lunch at the top of their lungs. If she skipped her own lunch, she could hunt up Smith right now.

When she offered to meet him within the hour, he flatly declined. "Perhaps tonight?" he suggested instead.

She wanted to give him "no" for a change. But if she put him off, Smith might hire someone else in the meantime, and she wouldn't find out what he was up to. "Okay," she said.

"Nine o'clock," he decided.

She could work her balloon deliveries around it. As she hung up the phone, the girls linked arms like ice skaters and rushed off, scraping pedestrians out of their path.

SHE STOPPED AT HOME for a snack before going to work. Hank, paying bills at the kitchen table, eyed the unimaginative peanut butter, butter and lettuce sandwich Kate was constructing.

"Wouldn't you like some green peppers or onion in that? Tomato, maybe? Pickles?"

"Mmphh," Kate muttered around an impolite mouthful. "Thish ish fine." She tucked a strand of lettuce back into the bread and swallowed. "Any mail for me? Phone calls?"

What she really meant was did Garrett relent and send me an urgent message to come, come, come to him? She sighed, to show she wasn't holding her breath.

"As a matter of fact," Hank said, laying down her pen to hunt the handkerchief out of her sleeve and dab her nose with it, "I don't believe so."

Kate's shoulders drooped. She chewed listlessly.

"You and Garrett Brody don't seem to communicate anymore," Hank said, eyes full of concern.

"Easy come, difficult go." Kate let sadness peep out for half a minute before stiffening her posture. "This sandwich *could* use a little horseradish or something," she decided finally.

"YOU AND KATE CHRISTOPHER don't seem to be an item anymore," Mac said, hefting his sneakered feet to his desktop and biting into a cold turkey sandwich. "Not my fault, I hope?"

"Not your fault," Garrett conceded, pretending to be engrossed in the telephone bill he was preparing to pay.

"You don't need to be afraid of me being a pest," Mac mumbled, his mouth full. "Feel free to have dates. I'll respect your privacy."

"I'll feel free."

"Uhh, Gare, just pick yourself another girl with a bod like Kate's."

Gritting his teeth, Garrett began to write the check with unnecessary roughness.

BETWEEN THE TIME SHE PRESENTED a spray of pink balloons to a new baby and the singing of a syrupy jingle for a golden wedding anniversary, Kate buzzed the red Honda toward Harvey Smith's address. The neighborhood got fancier the closer she came, lawns spreading out, iron fences springing up, vegetation thickening. She whistled a short, dying note as she cruised once past Smith's driveway, marked by a stucco gatepost and a gas lamp that should have had a country club sign attached to it.

Snaking around a cul-de-sac, she crept back to the entrance and through the open wooden gate. The asphalt under her tires was smooth as silk, leading her to the front door of a Colonial mansion, white colonnades and all. Kate parked and wiped a hand across her eyes, half expecting a liveried footman or hoopskirted belle to appear on the porch.

No one appeared. She ducked her head to peer up at the dark second-story windows, fluffed up her hair, checked her lipstick in the rearview mirror, and told herself to stop stalling. Her bunny suit, from which she'd been too stubborn to change, caught on the door handle, making her hop, awkwardly but appropriately, the first few steps. The costume head, left behind on the passenger seat looked, when she glanced back, like a skull with ears.

She walked five paces, then went back to her car and rummaged the Mace container out of the glove compartment. Tucking it into her wristband, she retraced the route she'd started.

The peals of the doorbell resounded deeply in the house. She stepped back, glad the night had turned cool enough for fur, and tried to look professional.

14

THE DOOR SWEPT OPEN and a heavyset man stood there inspecting her. "Ms. Christopher?"

"Yes. Mr. Smith?"

"Yes. Please come in."

They both waddled into the foyer, which was the size of a bungalow, and Smith twisted around to reexamine Kate in her bunny costume. His charcoal eyes betrayed no sense of humor whatsoever.

"If you'll just step into the library—"

He waved at a mahogany double door and Kate felt a thrill of excitement. She'd always wanted to see a real, posh, private library.

Crossing the threshold, Kate swiveled to tell him she wasn't disappointed by the room's size and decor, but he was gone.

The room was grand—a sea of oak flooring, dotted with Oriental rugs, rosy wood walls and ceiling, polished within an inch of their lives, a fieldstone fireplace hung with a buffalo trophy that looked as benign as her bunny head. And shelves of books. Tipping her head back to examine the titles, Kate found mostly geography, science and history, some cookbooks, some joke books, and at least one Mickey Spillaine.

Assuming he'd gone to get the silver tea service, she chose an intricately carved rocker and sat down, crossing her furry ankles.

Garrett would look wonderful in this room, she thought. Wearing a black tux and ruffled shirt, his hair slicked back and gleaming, a snifter in one hand and her satined waist in the other—

The door snicked open and a man too small to be Mr. Smith came toward the light. "Kate!" he welcomed, waving his cane.

"Mr. Garcia?" She could imagine her delusionary Garrett spilling the brandy down her cleavage when she started in surprise.

"How nice to see you," he said politely just before bellowing at the empty doorway, "Harvey, bring us coffee."

"Mr. Smith is your butler?" Kate relaxed back into her chair again and slowly rocked to show him she was taking it all in stride.

"My paid companion and unpaid friend." He perched on the arm of one boulder-shaped couch and rested the cane crossways on his knees. "I was just asking Dr. Brody about you this morning."

"Oh? And what did he say?" She fought down an impulse to bend forward and lock eyes with Mr. Garcia.

"Why, he was unusually brusque—didn't really answer me. Just muttered something about you not coming back because you'd lost interest."

Ha!

Mr. Garcia cocked his head, examining her. "But after Dr. Brody left the room, the young woman with the unfortunate hair—"

"Nicki."

"Nicki. She said it was a case of lover's spit."

"Mmm—you think she meant *spat*?"

Nodding and beaming, he lowered his voice. "I didn't realize that you and he, the two of you—"

"We didn't. Weren't. Well, we were, but now we aren't. But I would."

His face showed a brief but game attempt to untangle her "explanation." Shrugging, he said, "And now here you are, a magician. I didn't know that, either! You should have worn that outfit to the lab. Nicki would have been so envious of it."

Smith came sideways into the room with a wicker tray the size of a swinging gate. Huddled in the center of it were two stoneware mugs, two spoons, a yellow sugar bowl, a purple cream pitcher, and a jar of instant coffee. He set his load on a slab of occasional table and handed Kate her cupful of hot water.

"What did you say you do for a living?" she asked Mr. Garcia.

"I probably told you 'a little of everything.' I'm retired now. Aren't you having a cup with us, Harvey?"

Kate recognized the unadorned "No." That was Mr. Smith, all right.

As he exited, Mr. Garcia continued, "You're wondering how I made the money to own this place."

"Well, yes, nosy me." Organized crime had come to mind.

"My daddy was a ranch hand, Mama took in laundry, and I had five brothers and sisters. All gone now." He still, oddly, beamed. "I worked hard at a lot of different jobs—the air force, a private flying service, selling soap, selling real estate, promoting prizefights. A friend and I invented a floor wax that dries in five seconds. And along the way I was investing lucky and smart."

"No wife to help you spend it?"

Still beaming, he shook his head.

"And why are you interested in Garrett Brody and CROPS?"

"How old do you think I am, Kate?" He showed her both profiles, to help her decide.

She sipped at the coffee, which wasn't too hot in more ways than one, and picked, "Sixty, sixty-five."

His grin threatened to split his face. "I'm seventy-nine my next birthday."

"That's amazing," she said, meaning it. "You're much younger looking."

"Most times I feel younger, too. But I have to think about what to do with my millions when I die." He said "millions" as casually as Kate would have said "hundreds." Finally his smile flickered out.

"Is this where CROPS comes in?" she ventured.

"I've already allotted money to four excellent charities, and Harvey, of course, will be taken care of. But I'd like to contribute to some enterprise that will make a mark in history. Help a scholar discover or invent something that would swerve humankind onto a different course. Understand what I'm getting at?"

She nodded. "Proof of ESP or life after death would certainly do that."

"Wowie, yes!" He carefully set aside his still full cup and rested his hands on his knees. "So what do you think?"

"I think you hired Perry Strickland to snoop around the CROPS facilities to see if he could discover anything wrong with it."

"Smart lady," he said, pointing his cane at her to show whom he meant.

"And then you got the idea of a magician being able to detect better than a detective, in this case."

"Right again. What's so funny?"

"Mr. Smith obviously didn't tell Jamie Bing why you wanted to spy on CROPS. I can't wait to see his face when he finds out it was so you could endow the lab with a ton of money."

"That's assuming we don't find any evidence of sloppy research work," he reminded her sternly.

"Mr. Garcia, I was a total stranger to CROPS and Garrett Brody when I volunteered for tests about a month ago, and I went with the rather shabby intention of using my sleight of hand skills to falsify test results and convince everyone I was, indeed, psychic." She ran one finger inside her chafing collar. "I wasn't able to fake anything. Garrett and Mac never let their guards down. They keep everything locked up and confidential, from where the supplies are stored to where the results are filed. If they ever discover something they consider significant, you can believe, it *is* significant."

Fingertips to eyelids, Garcia meditated. Expelling a decisive breath, he looked over at her. "Think I should get a second opinion?"

She spread her hands. "It's your fortune."

"Hmm—mm." He thought some more. "Are you pretty good? Magic-wise?"

She stood up. "Got a couple quarters?"

For the next five minutes, she made two quarters seem like two dozen, having them appear and disappear and change into dimes and dollar bills. Garcia sat transfixed, a boy at the circus again, baffled and delighted. She brought the routine to a spectacular finish by returning the pocket watch and wallet he hadn't yet noticed were gone.

"With a talent like that, you won't ever go hungry," he exclaimed.

Instead of returning to her chair, Kate walked toward the door. "I better go. I've still got another telegram to deliver tonight."

"You and Dr. Brody. Is it serious?" He crossed his knees as if he was staying for a while. "Don't look at me like that. I'm old and rich enough to ask impertinent questions."

"It could have been serious, but it jumped the track when he found out I was a magician. If I had it to do over, I'd tell him the minute we met." She stuck out her chin and started toward the door again.

"Wait, wait." Garcia fumbled through his pockets and brought out a checkbook and a ballpoint pen adorned with advertising copy.

"You don't owe me anything, Mr. Garcia. I didn't do anything." She took another step in the direction of the exit.

"I was prepared to pay several thousand dollars for a job that might take months to complete." He stretched the checkbook open on his knee and began to write.

She kept walking. "No, really. I can't take it."

"Ms. Christopher—Kate—"

"You can donate it to Garrett's cause in my name! Thanks for an interesting hour," she called from the foyer, her voice echoing. Then she turned to the butler. "Thanks, Mr. Smith, I see the front door. I left a bread-crumb trail. Night."

Just a tickle of breeze soothed her flushed cheeks as she padded to her car. "You want to know what I just turned down?" she said, addressing the bunny head as she reached for the ignition. "Don't ask."

LIFE WENT ON. Kate worked, ate, slept, worked, ate, slept.

Minda convinced her to go on a blind date with a cousin from Hollywood. The guy looked like Jeff Bridges, drove like Mario Andretti, and danced like John Travolta. Unfortunately, he also reasoned like Ralph Kramden.

Four days after her interview with Rudy Garcia, Kate found a typewritten envelope from CROPS among the "You're-already-a-winner" mail. She laid it deliberately on the kitchen table while she poured herself a glass of orange juice, prolonging the suspense. Good news or bad? Maybe Garrett was going to sue her for disrupting his tests or causing his dog mental anguish.

Hank bustled in with her black handbag on one arm and a shopping bag slung on the other. "I've decided to make a dog."

Choking on orange juice—fruit acid scalding her throat—Kate wheezed, "How?"

Dropping the leather bag and upending the shopping bag over the table and Kate's letter, Hank answered, "Wire, tape, whatever it takes. If he turns out well, maybe you'd want to use him in the bunny box."

"A robot? I like it," Kate decided. She extracted her letter from the heap of junk on the table and carried it upstairs to read in private—in case its contents dragged some horrible expletive from her.

It said: Dear Kate, Rudy Garcia has made a gift of two thousand dollars to CROPS for ongoing studies in ESP. He stressed that the donation is made in your name, and that it was to you I should direct our thanks. Although I don't understand it, I do appreciate, deeply, your role in making this generous gift possible.

Very truly yours,
Garrett—handwritten,
Garrett Brody:—typed

She read it over two more times and still couldn't find the place where it asked her for a date. Quietly sighing, she reassembled the letter and envelope and tucked them, carefully, into the wastebasket.

ANOTHER WEEK STROLLED BY. Summer was well established now, with its sunny, hot days, and its starry, cool nights.

Jamie Bing had finally forgiven Kate, for the most part because he needed her to assist him in his act for a couple of weeks while Minda nursed her flu. As Kate shivered on air-conditioned stages, in black sequined shorts and fishnet stockings, she worried another cold was lurking in the wings, waiting for her.

But life went on.

The aunts, judging they had enough recipes in their book, sent introductory letters and sample chapters to publishing houses all over the United States and Canada. Replies began to come back, many of which cited, "Don't publish humor," as the reason for rejection.

Hank's robot dog was taking shape. Christened Tuffy II by Corliss, who was also sewing him a polyester fur coat, he spent most of his time in the middle of the kitchen table—an unappetizing centerpiece leaking wire and plastic entrails. Enthusiastic about her creation, Hank claimed she wanted to make a gorilla with a built-in vacuum cleaner next.

June ticked away with fireworks crackling at night and the sun a blast furnace by day. Denver's complicated lawn watering restrictions went into effect. The snowshoe bunny suit was packed away in favor of a cooler, desert breed. And there was always a foggy-sided pitcher of lemonade in the refrigerator.

When none of Kate's activities crossed paths with Mr. Garcia, Perry Strickland, Nicki or Mac—in or out of his body—their faces began to blur and fade.

Garrett's, however, never did. Like a microscope zooming in on a slide, Kate's mind's eye would isolate some portion of his face—the laugh lines at his eyes, the corner of his mouth as it lifted into a smile, the white flash of his teeth, the gray glint of a missed whisker—and she would have to hold her breath or hug herself against the sudden stab of pain.

"DO I HAVE THE GIRL FOR YOU," Mac boasted, throwing a brotherly arm around Garrett's shoulder blades as they walked along the lab's lower hall. "A stunner."

"If she's so fabulous, why aren't you taking her out yourself?"

"She's too tall for me. Besides, she's prejudiced against divorced men. Unless they're handsome. Or have plenty of money."

"She sounds like a great gal, all right," Garrett said, checking the lock on the sensory deprivation chamber and experiencing a memory flash of Kate stumbling into his arms.

"You aren't looking for a bride, are you?" Mac scolded, following Garrett toward the kitchen. "She'd just be fun to be with. Take your mind off your troubles."

"How come you're so eager to match me up lately?"

"I feel responsible for what happened between you two. It was right after I trespassed that you and Kate split up."

"It's not your fault, Mac. The lady is a magician. The enemy, *comprenez-vous?*"

Mac pretended to start back in horror. "A magician? Aaagh, a magician!"

Garrett stopped dead in his tracks. "What does this wonder woman you want me to meet do for a living?"

"She's a—what do you call it? Beautician."

"That's it? Just a woman that fixes other women's hair?"

Mac raised his voice in embarrassed protest. "Well, yeah, but—"

"Perfect. Give me her phone number."

ONE MORNING while Kate was wrestling the garden hose into a configuration that would sprinkle as much of the front lawn and as little of the neighbor's driveway as possible, Corliss floated behind the screen door to call her to the phone.

"A Rudy Garcia for you," Corliss amplified as Kate passed her in the hall.

"Hi, Mr. G.," Kate said, transferring a smear of mud from the heel of one hand to the seat of her cutoff jeans. "What's up?"

"My birthday. I'm having a few friends to a party at the house and I want to hire you to do a magic show."

Tipping the chair onto its rear legs, she stretched to see the wall calendar. "When?"

"The fourth of July."

"I should have known! It looks okay. What time do you want me?" Tuffy II had black button eyes now that stared balefully at her. She draped a paper napkin over his head.

"The party is from seven to whenever. Please feel free to come early and mingle. You have a friend or two on the guest list."

"Oh?" Her voice frowned, but her heart jumped to happy conclusions. "Like who, for instance?"

"Since you're such a bright lady, I'm sure you can guess. Wear your prettiest dress, and plan your most dazzling act."

"Funny, you don't look like a matchmaker." She rearranged Tuffy's napkin into a diaper, whisking transparent tape from a nearby dispenser to hold it in place. "It's nice of you to arrange this rendezvous, but don't get your hopes up, okay?"

"You haven't seen him walking around the lab like a zombie, snapping everyone's head off when he deigns to say something. This is one unhappy man, I guarantee it, and I don't have to be a detective or a magician to figure out why."

Smiling at the receiver, Kate purred, "Unhappy, huh?"

"Definitely." She could hear him smiling, too.

"See you on the fourth," she promised.

Before she went back to her yard work, Kate drank a glass of lemonade and, hearing Hank coming, dribbled the last of it into the napkin-diaper.

15

NEVER—NOT FOR TALENT SCOUTS in the audience or Hollywood producers—had Kate dressed so carefully for a performance. Her dress was new, low-cut and molded above the waist, floating below in a short, flirty skirt. The jacket, necessary for its deep pockets, was made of the same, pale and glittering beige. She wore ivory sandals with impossibly steep and slender heels, and fake diamonds that winked fire from each earlobe. Her hair, full and sun-streaked, was as soft as the dress and as shiny as the jewelry. Eyes and mouth she'd painted with the single-mindedness of a performer preparing to dazzle her audience.

It was a typical Colorado summer evening, dusk spreading like a cool balm after too much sun. Kate threaded through traffic with the careful preoccupation of an experienced driver on automatic pilot.

Just because Garrett had been invited didn't mean he'd come to the party. She must brace herself for possible disappointment.

And even if he did come to the party, it didn't necessarily mean he'd be happy to see her. He might not even speak to her. She screwed her shoulders straighter in the bucket seat and glanced haughtily at the yellow light she was sailing through.

The cul-de-sac looked like a Hollywood used car lot, full of sports cars and limousines. There was no use turning into the driveway with its tiki torches and intermittent fireworks. Kate found a space by nosing the little Honda to the curb and leaving it vulnerable to rear-swiping.

She clip-clopped along the sidewalk, up Rudy Garcia's marble stairs and into the foyer, her shoulders back and nostrils flaring like she owned the place. The first person she saw was Garrett. The second person she saw was Garrett's date.

She presumed that's who the tall, fashionably concave-chested woman with the improbably red mane was. They hadn't noticed Kate's arrival and as she hesitated in the living-room archway, she noted Garrett's sweetly serious expression, the hint of sorrow around his eyes, the unkempt haircut, the drooping shoulder—the strong hand that reached around "Red's" waist and gave her a quick, spontaneous squeeze.

"Kate!" Mr. Garcia announced loudly, and her eyes leaped away to her host, who was using his cane like a scythe to clear a path to her. "You look stunning! Beautiful! Gorgeous!"

"So do you," she said, tapping him on his baby blue cummerbund, no more able to keep her pretense at sophisticated aloofness than she could resist peeking over at Garrett again.

The redhead had her drinking arm intricately entwined with his, and her free hand inside his gray suit jacket, fondling his paisley tie. He dipped his face in Kate's direction in what was either a nod or a burp.

"Come have a drink and meet some people," Mr. Garcia said, pointing her into the living room, a fraternal twin to the library.

The party theme seemed to be combination patriotic and jungle. Red, white and blue buntings swooped from ceiling beam to ceiling beam. Huge potted palms and massive banks of multicolored flowers made Kate think uneasily of funeral parlors. Not a balloon was in sight.

Mr. Garcia's idea of a few friends was perhaps one hundred and fifty, and more were arriving. A live mariachi band erupted in one corner, and the conversational din increased correspondingly. Harvey Smith lumbered about offering drinks, running interference for three nubile ladies in black-and-white French maid attire, who were offering canapés and more drinks.

The muscles of her face aching in a frozen, radiant smile, Kate had lost her host and was drifting with the tides of the crowd, when a voice the texture of honey and gravel tickled her ear.

"You do look beautiful tonight."

"Thank you, Garrett," she answered, turning around to face him. "So does what's-her-face."

Garrett's escort's head leaned forward from his other side and shouted, "What?"

"Kate Christopher, Amaris Winslow," Garrett said.

Kate cupped an ear and repeated, "Avarice?"

"Amaris, Amaris." The other woman assured her, nodding and smiling as she yanked upward on a spaghetti strap just in time to avoid indecent exposure. There weren't any tattletale lines of underwear under the slinky white dress, maybe because it was, itself, a slip.

"How are your aunts?" Garrett asked, folding his arms and rocking on his heels like a church deacon waiting for the service to begin.

"Fine, fine."

"I'd still like to test them sometime. Ask them to give me a call," he said so pompously Kate wanted to punch him.

She decided to give him one more chance. "They may have a publisher for their book."

"Wonderful."

"That's if they can revise it to suit. The editor says some of the recipes aren't unusual enough."

"Poor guinea pig Kate!" He really laughed. She really grinned.

"What about pigs?" Amaris swayed between them to ask.

The band ended a set and burst into a new one, which, to Kate's untrained ear, might have been the same one all over again.

"Let's dance," Amaris insisted, bobbing up and down to the beat, polishing Garrett's jacket with her dress.

"Nice to have seen you again," Garrett said as Amaris towed him away.

Kate answered with a nasty smile. She couldn't imagine Garrett being seriously interested in a long-term relationship with a skinny airhead. On the other hand, Amaris probably thought talking plants and disembodied colleagues lent spice to a tumble in bed.

Mr. Garcia was crossing the room purposefully—his cane, as usual, less a crutch than a weapon. He motioned Kate to follow him into the foyer where the crowd thinned to two people per square yard.

"What do you need in the way of a stage?" he asked, a fatherly hand on her back.

"Maybe the band would let me use their little platform. I could do a short routine there and then just wander informally among your guests performing parlor tricks."

"No wallet stealing," he said, wagging a cautionary finger.

She went to retrieve her props from the car while Garcia went to chase the band off their stand.

HELPED BY AN APPRECIATIVE audience mellowed by Mr. Garcia's expensive liquor, Kate was giving the performance of her life. Acutely aware of Garrett in the front on her far right, she vanished and color-changed silks, cut and restored rope, transformed milk to flowers, and, with a mischievous nod at the parapsychologist, *divined* what number was showing on a pair of dice a volunteer had boxed.

As applause for this last trick receded, Kate asked Mr. Garcia, sitting front and center on a high-backed walnut dining chair, "May I borrow your driver's license?"

"Don't have one. Dr. Brody," he roared. "Give her your driver's license."

Amaris, giggling and clinging to his arm, made it difficult for Garrett to extract his wallet and select the required card. Amaris snatched it up and danced the short distance to hand it to Kate.

"Thank you. Hmm, did you know this expired in 1985? Wow, look at all these points on the back!" She smiled while the audience added jibes of their own to her teasing, and Garrett folded his arms, looking resigned.

"A matchbox," she said, holding it up. "Would you examine it, Mr. G.—" he did "—and tell us if it's absolutely empty?" It was.

Kate casually held Garrett's license for all to see in her left hand while her right dipped with equal casualness into her jacket pocket to palm the fake license.

To accept the approved matchbox that Mr. Garcia handed up to her, she made the natural transfer of license to right hand, and took the box in her left, saying, "Let's get rid of this horrible likeness of Dr. Brody. Let's just make it disappear."

Palming the real license, she flashed the ringer before dropping it into the box and shutting the lid. "The magic words for this are, 'get a horse.'" She slid the lid open, frowned, and showed that the box still contained a license. "Magic words aren't going to be enough for *that* bad a photograph. Anyone got a match?"

Before anyone in the snickering forefront could present one, she plucked her own out of thin air. Among her props was a fat, clear glass ashtray which she set ostentatiously on her portable worktable. Opening the box one more time to demonstrate the license was inside, she lit the match with a contemptuous flick of one fingernail—a graceful piece of business that had cost her a carton of matches, two fingernails, and a square inch of skin to perfect—and dropped the flame into the still gaping box. The fire flared and died to the crowd's appreciative murmur.

"Worried?" Kate asked Garrett, who shook his head and braced himself under Amaris's happily nervous clutches.

"If I'm worried, are you worried?" she persisted, pretending to search herself for licenses. "If I'm not mistaken—" She craned her neck to look around the room. "Is Mr. Smith here? Would someone send Harvey Smith up here, please?"

After a few moments of confused milling around, the audience found him, pushing him to the front, where Kate made him turn around and empty out his jacket pocket. As soon as the license appeared, she swept it away to offer to Garrett while applause swelled.

"Is that your driver's license?" she shouted smugly, and the noise abated expectantly.

At that moment the trick went sour. Garrett glanced at the license, did a double take, and, stabbing it inside his jacket, he gave her a sickly smile.

"Yep," he said. "Mine."

The applause resumed and Kate took an uncertain step backward.

Amaris squealed. "How'd she do that? Let me see?" She fought Garrett's hand away and hauled out the license. In a voice that would etch glass, she announced, "This isn't your picture. This is Pee-wee Herman!" and she began waving it around for confirmation.

Kate shrugged expressively at Garrett, her eyes thanking him for trying. Then she turned to the crowd. "Gee, I don't know what went wrong. Boy, don't you just wish sometimes you could run time in reverse and correct your mistakes?"

She held aloft the glass ashtray. "It might be worth a try, folks. Let's put the fire back in here and see if the license is restored with it."

She crumpled up a bit of flash paper, a chemically treated tissue that would live up to its name. Repeating the fingernail-to-match theatrics, she touched the paper and, as it whooshed and died, she snapped Garrett's license from her palm into the ashtray; the little card seemed to rise, phoenix-like, from the ashes.

To enthusiastic applause, she walked the real license over to Garrett and took the Pee-wee Herman one in exchange. For his ears only, she said, "Oh ye of little faith."

"Sorry. I almost messed up your trick."

"It was sweet, your wanting to protect me with a lie."

"I should have known Bing wouldn't send me someone clumsy enough to accidentally burn up a driver's license."

Amaris saved Kate from a cutting reply by pushing between them. "How on earth did you do that?"

"Practice."

"The lady is practiced to deceive," Garrett took an unworthy dig, then smiled as if his comment was meant in fun.

"Kate, is that all?" Mr. Garcia called, and didn't wait for an answer. "Kate is going to walk among you and surprise you with other marvelous illusions. There's a poker game starting in the library for all interested cardsharps. Kate, you aren't invited."

Washed by the good-humored remarks of the disintegrating crowd about her talent, she gazed after Garrett's stiff back and Amaris's creamy, naked one. With superhuman effort, she kept her tongue in her mouth.

Many coins and bills vanished, materialized, and changed during the next four hours, but none of them were Garrett's. He and Amaris had disappeared shortly after his license to drive was restored. Kate wished her repertoire included invoking a thunderstorm. The best she could do was a gypsy curse—*give 'em hell, Smedley.*

RUDY GARCIA INSISTED ON paying her a bonus. It was one o'clock in the morning when he wrote the check, having brought her into the relative quiet of the kitchen to do it. She glanced around the chrome-and-butcher-block room with its yards and yards of counter and shelf space and pictured her aunts turned loose here with their bags of groceries and rampant imaginations.

"You and Garrett Brody didn't have much time together tonight," he said, ripping loose the check and waving it dry.

The band, improved by the muffling walls, played one more song, identical to the preceding ones. Kate bet the party would still be in full cry when Mr. Garcia gave up and went to bed.

"You're a matchmaker all right," Kate chided. "But you're going to have to admit defeat on this one. I hurt his pride. Obviously he's not a forgiving man."

"Maybe in time." He handed her the check and massaged his belly under the restrictive cummerbund.

"Maybe. But why should I wait around? I've got pride, too." She disguised the bitterness with a smile. "Have you told him about the endowment yet? I mean the big one?"

"No." Garcia yawned hugely, revealing a fortune in gold fillings. "I'm still working out the details."

"But you are going to do it—leave CROPS some money?" The yawn was contagious, as they always are, and Kate's eyes watered with the effort to squeeze it in.

"If you still think everything is copacetic at the lab. I'd sure hate to leave my fortune to a gang of mismanaged slubberers."

"Oh, I'm sure Garrett doesn't, uh, slubber." She stood and patted his liver-spotted fist resting across the checkbook.

"Did he thank you for the two thousand I gave in your name?" he asked, temporarily trapping her wrist.

"He wrote me a very nice letter, yes, thank you."

"Letter! Phaw. The man *is* an idiot." He shook her hand gravely before letting loose. "Here I am an eligible bachelor, and there he is an eligible idiot. Women! Go figure."

"I'm going," she announced, suddenly aware of her spiked-shoed feet feeling as if they'd been slammed in a door. "Happy birthday."

She drove home barefoot and spent the rest of what was left of the night scrambling the covers of her bed, remembering Garrett's handsome head bent attentively toward Amaris, and visualizing Garrett's handsome head resting on a pillow emblazoned with a spill of hot red hair. . . .

16

KATE DID DUTIFULLY PASS ALONG Garrett's invitation to her aunts, fully aware they knew of her estrangement from him and would therefore never call him out of loyalty to her.

Less than a week later she arrived home from work one night to find them in their best clothes, perfumed and powdered, having spent the day at CROPS.

"Why didn't you tell me you were going? I could have driven you out there," she scolded more severely than was warranted.

"That's all right," Corliss said, tying a red-flowered apron over her pink-flowered dress. "Garrett picked us up and Mac brought us home."

The aunts began to bang utensils and run water, too busy to talk to her.

"So how did you do?" Kate asked insistently.

"Oh, just terrible," Hank announced, as proudly as if she'd said, "just great."

"Terrible in what way?" Kate took the potato peeler away from her and picked up the first potato.

"In every way," Corliss said, smiling complacently.

Kate gasped with what she was afraid was comprehension. "Were you trying to sabotage Garrett's tests?"

"Oh, no, dear," Hank said. "We wouldn't do that. It's just that—"

"The tests were too easy," Corliss finished. "And some of them we answered correctly but our correct answers were different from the correct correct answers."

Kate saw that she'd whittled the big potato down to the size of a small egg. "Tell me from the beginning."

"Well, let's see. First it was the colors test."

Corliss nodded, setting the table.

"Have you done that one, Kate? Where you put your arms in a box? Okay, we each did that, only I couldn't do it at all, and Corliss was too specific."

"Too specific?"

"Yes. Garrett didn't like it when she called yellow 'canary,' or the red 'scarlet.' Then, they had an argument about what 'mauve' is."

"A polite disagreement," Corliss corrected. "He says he'll get a wider variety of colors for me to identify next time."

Hank was slicing cheese, one for the plate, one for herself, one for the plate, one for herself. "So then he put me in the solitary confinement—"

"Sensory deprivation."

"—and kept Corliss in Testing. And she'd look at these different objects he gave her to handle, trying to send me a mental picture, and I'd say whatever came into my head."

"Which was way off the mark sometimes." Corliss helped herself to cheese; the plate was losing ground.

"How could I have been holding an automobile tire, for goodness sake?"

"It was the headphones. Their swishing sounded like a leaky inner tube."

"What did you want to do with these potatoes?" Kate asked, showing them to Hank.

"I was going to fry them, but maybe we should hard-boil them."

"Sorry. Go on with your story."

"I did say that the apple was some kind of fruit and the sponge was a soft, holey blob. But then I said the pencil was a tree."

"But that's wonderful, Hank," Kate exclaimed. "You were going all the way back to the origin of the pencil."

"Garrett said that was probably what happened, but it didn't help him score it."

"Or the handkerchief that you called a bush," Corliss ticked off her fingers. "Or the ring you said was a rock. Or the glue stick you thought was a horse."

Kate had to sit down to laugh. "I wish I could have seen Garrett's face!" The thought was sobering. She really did wish she could see Garrett's face. It was awful to be jealous of her aunts. "So what else did you do?"

"He had us stare at a pen on a graph in a fishbowl."

"And?"

"We sat there fifteen minutes with our wires crossed. Corliss was trying to make the pen go down and I was trying to make it go up, so of course we didn't move it at all."

Kate hugged herself in a fresh spasm of giggles.

Hank shielded her eyes with one hand and picked out two spices at random from the rack on the wall. She glanced at them before sprinkling the potatoes.

"Are you going back?" Kate asked.

"Well, Garrett very politely invited us, but—"

"We think we could set up our own experiments right here at home—"

"To save time. And then we could maybe do a sequel to *Cooking Without a License*—"

"Called *Communicating Without a Word.*"

Everyone considered this in appropriate silence till Hank turned from the stove and beamed at Kate. "Dr. Brody asked about you."

"He did?" She tried to ignore the little jab of pleasure.

"Oh, yes. He asked how you happened to get mixed up with that pompous peabrain Bing. Did I get that right, Corliss?" Getting a nod, she continued, "So we told him you answered Bing's cattle drive."

"I believe it's called cattle call," Corliss interjected.

"Yes, and we also told him you'd always been interested in magic, even as a little tyke."

Kate's pleasure rapidly faded into apprehension. "You did."

"And about how you loved to go to a magic show, but you were always so scared of clowns—"

Kate wanted to cover her ears.

"—you wet your pants at the circus."

"I bet Garrett thought that was fascinating, huh?" Kate said with dull resignation.

"Well, he's a psychologist, after all," Corliss said, reaching into the freezer compartment for ice. "He understands those kinds of things. Although I did think it odd when he asked if it had happened this year."

GARRETT WAS SILENTLY communicating with Fred as he gently polished the heart-shaped leaves.

You remember the great-looking lady I had in here a couple months ago? he thought. Kate? Turned out you were right to be leery of her. She had more up her sleeve than a shapely arm. Worst of it is, even now, knowing what she is, I miss her and want her and think of her all the time.

He attached the galvanometer to a gleaming leaf and straightened his back. *There you go, Fred. Listen, buddy, don't ever grow too close to Flo. Women are nothing but trouble.*

The monitoring pen on its treadmilling paper swooped with sympathy.

The telephone interrupted this exercise in self-pity. Dropping crossways on the splashing mattress, Garrett stretched to pick up the receiver.

"Dr. Brody, Rudy Garcia. We need to make an appointment to talk over some very important business."

NEXT DAY, A TUESDAY, Kate came home early in the afternoon, planning to spend the rest of the day barefoot, with lemonade, and a book on the porch swing. No one needed telegrams, balloons, or magic tricks till one o'clock Wednesday. She felt like a school kid on a teachers' conference day.

As she squeaked open the front screen door, Hank called from deep in the house, "Wait a minute. Wait right there."

Obediently, Kate stopped, eyeing the floor for signs of fresh wax. Another distant sound began to grow, a peculiar mixture of guttural cries and dull thuds. Alarmed that an intruder had Hank by the throat, Kate disregarded orders and hurried up the hall.

She and the noise converged outside the kitchen door. The thumping was four spastic feet on the hardwood floor, and the choking was a tape playing a canine impersonation of Hitler. Tuffy II staggered past her, blindly welcoming her home, the glass strapped to his neck erupting lemonade every time he succeeded in taking one more jolting step.

From the middle of the kitchen, Hank pointed a remote control box at his gyrating tail. When she hit buttons, the box jerked like a recoiling pistol. Tuffy, true to his namesake, continued to wander on obliviously.

"He still has some fleas to be worked out," Hank said.

"Bugs," Corliss corrected unnecessarily from the rocking chair. She was mending silks again, her lap a jumble of primary colors.

"Did I get mail or phone calls?" Kate asked out of habit. She reached into the refrigerator for orange juice, Tuffy having apparently depleted the lemonade.

"You had one call. Dr. Brody."

The carton of juice slipped two inches lower in her grasp. "Oh?" She opened the steamy-warm dishwasher and took out the first thing at hand, not noticing it was a plastic measuring cup that only accepted four tablespoons of juice. She sipped and thought.

"He said he'd call back."

As if on cue, the phone rang. Kate wiped juice off her nose and lifted the receiver. A disgustingly cheerful voice announced, "Hi, I'm Bobby, the survey robot, with just a few quest—"

Kate hung up. "It was for Tuffy," she said, putting down the cup to go upstairs and take off some clothes. At the front door, the furry robot was tirelessly trying to burrow outside.

MYSTERY NOVEL RESTING ON her stomach, legs and neck at awkward angles, swing barely swaying, Kate had fallen asleep. She often dreamed of Garrett, and here he was center stage in her dream. Mouth lifting at the corners in the shy, sly smile uniquely his. Hair dark and curling in the heat. Gray eyes glinting in the dying sun. Long, tanned fingers reaching out to stroke her skin....

His touch on her bare shoulder made her own mouth glide into a smile. "Kate?" his quiet voice soothed her ear. "Kate, do you know a dentist could adjust your bite so you wouldn't grind your teeth like that?"

Like window shades, her eyes snapped open. Garrett was standing by the swing, hand drawing back from shaking her awake. He was just as desirable as in her dream, though his amorous dialogue needed work.

"What time is it?" she asked, throwing her feet on the floor and yanking her halter straight.

"Nine-ish." He retreated to the porch railing and straddled it.

There was still enough light for Kate to be embarrassed by her skimpy clothes, mussed hair, and, undoubtedly, runny makeup. "You said you'd phone," she accused.

"I decided what we needed to discuss ought to be done in person. So you couldn't hang up on me."

"This sounds promising. Would you like a little wine to loosen your tongue?"

"No, thank you. I want to get this over—"

"Excuse me. Wait." She sent the swing into orbit, as she hopped up. Wrenching open the screen door she hurried in. "Something I have to do," she shouted. "Stay."

He probably thought I needed to use the bathroom, she grumbled to herself as she used comb and eye shadow and slipped on a blouse. Squirting perfume toward her pulse points, and immediately wishing she hadn't done something that obvious, she hip-hopped back downstairs and out onto the porch.

Garrett now sat on half of the swing. She settled gingerly into her half and waited.

"Rudy Garcia," he began. "He's very wealthy."

"I know."

A car went past on the street, trailing Def Leppard at the top of its stereo lungs.

"He's going to endow CROPS with close to a million dollars when he dies."

"I know."

"On one condition."

Two or three blocks away, Def Leppard seemed to be lost and circling.

"I don't know about the condition," Kate said, watching twilight puddle up in the corners of the porch. "He did ask my opinion on how tight a ship you run." She swiveled toward him, grinning. "Did you kick Perry Strickland out and tell him never to darken your door again, like you did me?"

"Hardly. Perry Strickland is licensed to carry a gun. All you've got is a wizard's permit, or something."

He laid his hand casually on the seat between them. Kate stuck both of hers under her thighs.

"So what's the condition?" she prodded.

Garrett cleared his throat unhappily. "I have to hire—CROPS has to keep a resident—to make sure all the testing is on the up-and-up—"

"A magician! Oh, that clever little man!" Kate freed one hand to punch Garrett's shoulder, crowing. "I love it!"

"Gee, maybe you'd rather I come back some other time, since you're feeling so weak and depressed," Garrett pretended to complain.

Kate kicked the swing into action. Its rhythmic scrape was the only sound, now, in the early night. The perfume of a neighbor's honeysuckle wafted by, momentarily overpowering the scent of Kate's perfume.

While she waited expectantly for Garret's apology and/or proposition, he lapsed into an interminable, thoughtful silence. Or fell asleep. It was the quietest, most peaceful twenty minutes they'd ever managed to spend together. Just as she was about to doze off again herself, Garrett's hand crept onto her knee and traced it lightly.

"You wanted another chance," he said without one ounce of romantic inflection.

"What are you trying to tell me, Garrett?" Her voice emerged a few degrees above freezing. "Now that Mr. Garcia endorses me, you're going to magnanimously forgive me? Money certainly does wonders for a relationship."

"Do you want the job or not?" His tone conveyed as much tenderness as Bobby, the survey robot's.

Slapping his hand away, Kate straightened, making the swing shudder to a stop. "Whose idea was it to offer it to me?"

"What the hell does that matter?"

"Thank you. You've answered the question quite succinctly."

"Rudy just suggested the same thing I would have thought of eventually. Probably. That I might as well hire a *pretty*—"

"Ahhrr! Pretty has nothing to do with talent. You're supposed to respect my skill."

"I do, I do!" He caught her hand back. "I never knew a trickier woman."

She gave up. Sitting in silence, letting him play with her fingers, she tried to decide whether she wanted to hit him or hug him.

Eventually he tired of just touching fingers and tried to move on to greater challenges. She put up token resistance for around two minutes, and then relaxed against his chest, concentrating on the pleasurable sensations she felt inside as his hands explored outside.

Feeling that she ought not to let him off too easily, she murmured, "Won't Amaris be jealous?"

"Amaris?" He sounded guilelessly astonished—which told Kate all she wanted to know about *that*.

When he fitted his mouth below her earlobe, she whispered, "Does this mean I've got the job?"

"Yesss," he lipped down her throat and across her collarbone.

"Easiest damn interview I ever had." She buried one hand in his thick, soft hair and gently dragged his head up for a kiss. Her tensed body relaxed and then tensed again in an entirely different way.

Garrett drew back his face enough to say, "When can you start?"

"I'm doing the best I can, Garrett," she muttered and was rewarded with his laugh. "Oh, you mean at the lab?"

The light in the hall came on, spilling a yellow delta on the porch floor. Tuffy barked for thirty seconds probably from the kitchen, and was cut off in mid-arf.

"You got a dog?" Garrett asked, kneading her backbone.

"Sort of. How about Friday morning?" She slipped fingers inside his shirt to fondle the warm skin and crisp hair there. "It's not a full-time job, right? I could work my usual afternoon and evening hours for Up and Away and doing magic?"

"You do magic, all right," he didn't answer her question. "That's, mmm—"

"Hello, ladies," a voice hailed from the direction of the street. Mr. Bledsoe and Pepper were out for a walk, and he'd seen the human shapes on the porch swing.

"Hello, Mr. B.," Kate called.

Pepper, off his leash, made a sweep of the front lawn, smelling the grass. He paused three-legged to stare at them for so long, Garrett guiltily withdrew his hand from Kate's bare thigh. Then Bledsoe whistled and the dog snuffled off.

"Friday morning's fine," Garrett said, replacing his hand, but a good two inches higher. "You didn't ask me about the wages."

"It's the fringe benefits that *really* interest me."

Tuffy II began to bark again, a yipping as annoyingly monotonous as any real canine's. About the same time, the telephone shrilled in almost perfect counterpoint. *Arp!* Ring. *Arp!* Ring. *Arp!*

The ringing stopped, and Hank's voice cut through the barks to ask Corliss if she'd seen Kate. A shadow blotted the light on the floor, and, sighing, Kate extracted her hand from Garrett's shirt. Just as Corliss angled open the screen door, Hank warned too late, "Don't let the dog out," and the yapping robot escaped onto the porch.

An answering burst of barking from the lawn indicated that Mr. Bledsoe and Pepper were on their return trip. Pepper knew this block like the back of his paw, and the only animals living at this house were three female humans. With bravery beyond the call of duty or good sense, he rushed to attack the strange breed now tumbling headfirst down the steps.

Corliss switched on the overhead porch light just in time for everyone to see Pepper lock jaws on Tuffy's neck and rip his head off. Mr. Bledsoe and Garrett froze, horrified. The two old ladies burst into laughter. Kate put her face into her hands and longed for desert islands.

17

AFTER THE FIRST FLUSH of exultant victory, Pepper dropped his oily-tasting enemy, who was still, unbelievingly, barking, though the tone had gone from bass to an Alvin Chipmunk tenor. Mr. Bledsoe and his pet exchanged baffled looks.

"It's okay, it's only a toy," Hank assured them.

"Only a toy," Kate echoed to Garrett as she pried his convulsive grip free of her leg. "Am I wanted on the phone?"

"Oh, my goodness, yes." Hank accepted Tuffy's remains from a still stricken Bledsoe. "It's a gentleman by the name of Nick."

Expecting to be offered aluminum siding or an exciting package of portraits of her loved ones, Kate snatched up the receiver and announced, "This is Kate."

"And this is Nicki," came with equal curtness down the wire. "Listen, I've been having this really bad psychic vibration about Garrett. He's there with you, right?"

"Yes, as a matter of—"

"Thought so. I should have asked for him in the first place." Chewing gum crackled, and, in the middle distance, several gunshots; Kate hoped it was only the TV.

"If you want to speak to Garrett, I'll get him," she offered without enthusiasm.

"You can give him a message, I guess. Tell him I get this strong impression of him being attacked by some kind of wild animal."

Kate rolled her eyes. "Like a dog maybe?"

"Could be. And tell him his car's probably got a tire going flat."

"My gosh, Nicki. You can actually tell that with ESP?"

"Naw. I noticed the broken bottle after he left his parking space this morning."

A FEW MINUTES LATER Kate was holding the flashlight while Garrett changed the tire. It wasn't romantic, but it was an activity they successfully engaged in with no interruptions whatsoever.

THE LITTLE RED HONDA seemed to find its own way up the highway and into the driveway to the parking lot where the only other car in evidence was Garrett's station wagon. When she'd cut the motor, Kate sat for a moment, looking at the Victorian lab that was to be her responsibility to police. What a cushy job—watching Garrett!

She bounced free of the seat and slammed the door, wanting to skip, instead of walk, to the building. The warm sun filtered through her hair and clothes. She spotted a daytime moon glowing wanly like someone's forgotten porch light. The petunias guarding CROPS's entrance bobbed in the breeze. In this absolutely perfect moment, stepping across the threshold seemed symbolic of the new direction Kate's life was taking.

"Hullooo!" she warbled happily. "Ready or not, here I come."

She'd worn a trim, black suit, very businesslike except for the frivolous, enameled Minnie Mouse pinned to the lapel of her jacket. Her two-inch heels clumped on the floor, as, walking down the hall, she looked in at open doors, beginning to feel a frisson of déjà vu.

Reaching for the front entry with its sweep of dual staircase, she paused, hand on the newel post and called, "Garrett?" remembering her nervousness when Mac had answered her greeting so many weeks ago.

"In the office," came the faint response now, and Kate climbed the stairs with an entirely different flutter in her stomach this time.

"Hi," she rejoiced, posing in the doorway for him to drink in her beauty.

"In a minute," he mumbled without looking up from the sheaf of papers in his hand.

She moved into the room, checked the set of an oak chair with a swipe of her forefinger, and sat down. Mac's desk was empty except for the typewriter and a white mug etched with a coffee ring. Garrett's desk looked like an overflowing Dumpster. He'd cleared a three-foot square to rest his elbows on while he worked. Dust motes floated and sparkled in the rays of sun.

Kate sneezed.

"In a minute," Garrett repeated, turning a page.

It felt more like a day. Kate mentally rearranged all the furniture, added a partition, took out the partition and put in a screen, painted the walls pale yellow and hung ivory brocade drapes before he finally looked up.

"Good morning," he said. "Article I'm writing for a psychology journal. You can check it over for me when it's finished."

"Sure." She reinstated the smile now that she had his attention, but he looked away before she had it up to full power. "Where is everybody?"

"Um, Mac went to see his folks. Body and all. Driving. This isn't Joe's day to clean."

Kate bit her tongue and said nothing.

"No testing scheduled this morning. Just you and I."

She squinted at his mouth, trying, unsuccessfully, to see a leer. "What have you got planned?" she asked, still optimistic.

Garrett dropped his pen and leaned back, lacing fingers behind his head. "All our testing procedures are documented, so you can go over them for loopholes. You should snoop around the storage areas for carelessness in supply handling. There are plenty of records from nearly two years' testing you should go over with a fine-tooth comb. And there are this week's test results that haven't been judged yet."

Garrett droned on about wages, hours, and benefits, his eyes fixed on the transom of the hall door. Feeling like a first grader who'd suddenly discovered school was not all coloring and recess, Kate crossed her knees and stared at her swinging toe.

You ninny, she scolded herself. This is a serious responsibility and you're here to do real work. Just because Garrett's your boss doesn't mean the job description includes hugs, kisses, and suggestive dialogue.

Underlying this lecture to herself was a growing worry that all had not been forgiven. That he would never let her back into his private life again.

"Okay?" he finished, and she nodded, hoping his previous sentence hadn't been "I'm going to take a nap while you scrub down the rest rooms."

Apparently what he'd said was she could use Mac's desk, because he stood up and shoved the typewriter to one side and opened a drawer for her to put her purse.

For the next two hours, Kate read and studied and judged. Then Garrett told her to take a ten minute break, which she did, alone in the kitchen with a cup of coffee and a stale donut. Next she inventoried supplies and considered how they were stored. And she took a self-guided tour of the building, all except for the attic and the basement which, from the top of the stairwell, evoked images she'd first encountered in Edgar Allan Poe.

GARRETT STOOD AT THE office window, staring blindly at the wild meadow, listening to the faint rustlings of Kate exploring the building. It hadn't been easy to keep his businesslike distance, this morning. He hadn't considered how difficult it would be to work side by side with her and keep his hands to himself. How could he continue to be polite and impersonal, discussing probability factors and controlled variables, when he craved to whip off clothes—his and hers—to get next to and inside her?

Ahh, she was tempting and fun. Was he ready to be bulldogged into a long-term commitment? Or—horrible thought—maybe he was ready and Kate wasn't planning on doing any bulldogging. His eyes followed a pair of hawks performing a stately dance against the clouds, so beautiful he wanted to cry.

In the distance, the antique clock tolled noon, and closer, Kate's light heels clacked on the stairway. Crossing the room to sit at his desk and open the first book that came to hand, Garrett waited for the soft scent of her, her lilting voice, wondering what she'd say and what he'd answer.

KATE USED THE BANISTER to help her up the last four risers, suddenly tired and discouraged. Garrett had forgiven her to the extent of hiring her, but not the extent of wanting her. The night on the porch swing had been lust, pure and simple. Well, not so pure.

Rounding the door, she went to Mac's desk without looking toward Garrett's, shrugged into her jacket, and said to the ceiling, "I'm going now."

He shot his sleeve up to look at his watch. "That late already? How about lunch? What time do you have to be back in Denver?"

"About 4:15," she answered abruptly.

"I brought lunch for two, in case." The first real smile he'd worn all day took the starch out of her spine; she smiled, too, before following him down the hall to the back stairs.

It wasn't peanut butter in a brown bag. It was cheese and fruit and wine and crisp French rolls in a wicker basket.

"A picnic?" Kate wondered aloud, so they took it and the kitchen table's oilcloth outdoors to the shady north side, where a grouping of low boulders formed a Neolithic table and chairs. They sat on the same rock, not touching, the basket between them.

Garrett scanned the sky, wanting to point out the hawks, but the only birds in sight were blue jays quarreling in a ponderosa pine. Frowning, he worked open the wine and took the first swig.

A gust of air swirled Kate's hair. "I didn't cheat on the remote viewing tests we took this spring," she said, folding her arms.

Offering her the bottle and a paper cup, he said, "I know. Which means you may really have some psychic talent. Your scores were significant, after all."

"Coincidence." She took the bottle and drank as he had, wiping her mouth with the back of one hand. "But it would be fun to explore it some more."

"Not while you're the lab's watchdog. Conflict of interest."

"How about my aunts?" She grinned maliciously. "Could they test some more without it being conflict of interest?"

"Interesting, it would be, no question. And there would undoubtedly be conflict. Something weird that no logical scientist could ever explain would happen. You'd better let me think about it."

They ate slowly, without further conversation, each gazing in a different direction as if lost in thought, each very conscious of the other—until a stroke of wind scattered the picnic leftovers, and the flapping tablecloth sent the wine bottle slopping across their laps. Out of nowhere, as the sun was still blithely shining, a tiny cloud relieved itself on their rock.

They locked eyes with each other and mutual laughter bubbled up. Shaking his head, Garrett dabbed ineffectually at Kate's skirt with a napkin and was considerably sobered by the sensuous feel of her thigh.

Her happy voice tickled in his ear. "Even when we aren't trying to make love, there are all these interruptions!"

Instead of taking this perfect opportunity, Garrett leaned away to his own side of the rock and absentmindedly lifted the empty bottle to his lips.

"You haven't forgiven me," she accused, the pain like a poof of flash paper. "You still resent that I meant to deceive you."

The corners of his mouth turned down. "I'm not a vindictive man, Kate." He began to gather up their trash.

"You're human, is all. You trusted me, I hurt you, and now you're wary of letting me get too close again."

"What is this?" he asked stiffly. "You're angry because I didn't fawn all over you this morning? You were hired as an auditor, not a call girl." He yanked up the basket and began to stride away.

"See? See how defensive you are?" She hounded him around the house. "What would've been wrong with a friendly hug when I came in this morning? Or even just a big, welcoming smile? A touch on the hand without jerking back like I'd burned you?"

His feet banged the back porch and he stomped through the door ahead of her. "I didn't know you were so sensitive! Or so demanding." Thumping the basket on the kitchen table, he whirled around like a karate fighter about to ward off a blow.

Kate strolled into the room, arms crossed, and favored him with a superior smile. "You better forgive me one hundred percent, or this relationship—professional and personal—is doomed. I don't want to be reminded, every time we have a disagreement, that I made that initial dumb mistake of trying to undermine your work."

"Kate." He spread his arms but didn't move to take her into them. "It's done. Your record is clean. What can I do to make you believe me?"

"I'm not sure," she said, pinning him with a meaningful glare. "Surprise me."

Several rooms away, a telephone began to ring. She threw up her hands in exasperation, grabbed her purse from a chair, and left the kitchen, the house, and Garrett, his face slack with disapproval.

When the phone call turned out to be a wrong number, Garrett uncharacteristically snarled at the caller and slammed down the receiver. Hands on his waist, he stared at the worn floor and his own scarred canvas shoes as he slowly climbed the stairs to the office.

So okay, he did feel residual resentment for Kate's treacherous intentions. After all, if she'd succeeded, his career would have been a shambles—all the years of conscientious work blown to hell. Of course it had taken a while to get over the shakes that thought gave him. What did she expect?

He sat down at his desk, uncapped a ballpoint pen, and forced himself to do some of the work he allegedly loved.

KATE KNEW SHE WOULDN'T BE depressed forever, but at the moment, scuffing up the sidewalk to her front porch, purse in one hand and shoes in the other, she felt mighty blue. Reaching to open the screen door, her hand was frozen by the sudden screech of an irritated infant.

Hank's voice rose above the wail, "Here it is, Jim-Jim," and the house hushed.

"Hello?" Kate stepped into the hall and scanned the floor for robot babies.

"In the kitchen. Come see our latest project," came the answering call.

Hank stood in the center of the room, hugging a shoe box to her stomach. Corliss sat in the rocker hugging a big-eyed baby.

"Baby-sitting?"

Kate crossed to admire their visitor and ground to a halt a yard from her goal. The tiny head sported wispy pale hair, a gravely sweet face, and a handlebar mustache.

"It's a pacifier!" she confirmed, laughing. "Your invention, ladies?"

"It's a *sassy-fier,*" Hank corrected. "We've designed several different ones." She dipped into the box. "Kitty whiskers. Glamour girl lips. Bunny rabbit teeth. Clown mouth—oh, sorry, Kate."

"How cute! So do you have marketing lined up?"

"Well, we just got these protocols in."

"Prototypes," Corliss corrected. "And we thought we'd take them around the local department stores to see if we could solicit some orders. Jim-Jim here is our neighbor across the alley. His mom is going to let him be our model."

Jim-Jim began to pedal a nonexistent bicycle and mutter. Corliss kicked the rocker into high gear.

"It's a great idea," Kate said, feeling a sappy urge to cry. She loved them, loved being with them, and hoped they'd never grow old.

"This one's my favorite," Hank said. The sassy-fier she dangled at Kate was a happy face mouth with two tiny Dracula fangs.

CALLING IT A DAY at four o'clock, Garrett trudged through shadows and dust to his station wagon. Kate had left him something on the front seat, a single, miniature balloon tied to a stick with silver and gold ribbons. With it was a note written on the back of one of her business cards: Sorry seems to be the hardest word.

His eyes sharpened on the odd, beige balloon and realized what it really was. It had come from a drugstore and belonged in a nightstand. Rereading the note, he gave up and laughed.

18

KATE HADN'T GIVEN UP. She'd just have to be perfect for the next few weeks. Drumming her fingers on the steering wheel while waiting for the traffic light to change, she psyched herself up for the task of winning over Garrett, trying to make him forget the past.

She'd have to wear her most becoming clothes, be vigilant of her hair, makeup, manicure. Be witty. Be cheerful. But most of all, be so seductive he couldn't stand it.

Was he worth the trouble? Was he! She pictured his expressive mouth, thick dark hair, strong arms and legs, his wide chest, his—

The car behind made a rude noise, pointing out the light was green. To demonstrate she was already in her good behavior mode, Kate gave the driver a friendly wave and gunned the motor.

She pulled to the curb near Up and Away and went in to report for duty. Jan sat at her desk—cigarette, coffee, and crossword at the ready; Doretta, obviously on her way home with briefcase and sweater, was reaching across the other desk to talk into the phone.

"Here she is now," she said, lifting her chin to signal Kate.

Feeling a rush of anticipation, Kate made her hello low and sultry, and slumped when it was Bing's voice she heard.

"Job for you, Great Kathy. This is absolutely the best opportunity I've found for you yet. The thrill of a lifetime."

"Mmm-hmm." She yawned deliberately into the receiver. "I'm listening."

"The Soviet Union," he intoned, then paused as if waiting for applause.

"I've heard of it. So?"

"How'd you like to *see* it? And get paid to do it?"

"Gee, Bing, I don't know. I sort of had my heart set on Antarctica, if I ever took my act on the road."

Bing knew her well enough to ignore her banter. "State department cultural exchange. In October. We'd be part of a vaudeville troupe."

"Why me? I thought you'd sworn off doing me favors." She put one hip on the desk and examined the manicure she'd resolved to overhaul.

"Minda has classes. The temporary employment service doesn't have any magician's assistants. That leaves you."

Maybe Bing actually enjoyed bickering with her. But then, he probably thought this particular proposal was no contest. She could picture his frustrated face when she told him, "No, I don't think so, thanks anyway."

"You're turning down a trip to Russia?" She had to hold the phone away from her ear and grimace at the other ladies. He continued to roar, "What do you mean 'no?' We haven't even discussed money yet. I used to think you were a bright, savvy, promising—"

"Captain, I love it when you compliment me," she interrupted before he could reach the meat of his sentence. "But I have other commitments." She hoped that was true.

"Fine. Maybe the new girl I hire to go to Russia with me will just kind of ease you out of a job."

"I could understand that, Bing," she said, suddenly sad that a longstanding relationship might really be coming to an end.

He hung up on her. For a moment, she itched to dial him back, tell him she'd changed her mind. If Garrett didn't succumb to her charms, didn't welcome her back into his life, she was going to need something like a trip to Europe to help her over the torturous disappointment.

Sighing, she turned to Jan. "What you got for me tonight?"

DURING THE NEXT THREE HOURS, Kate delivered five balloon bouquets, sang four jingles, smiled till her face ached, and did it all on automatic pilot, her mind otherwise engaged. One minute she was sure Garrett had meant to ask her for a date this weekend and her sudden departure from the lab had forestalled it. Next minute she was overwhelmed with the depressing conviction that she should have agreed to going on the Russian tour.

The mental turmoil was more tiring than the physical work, and she shuffled into Up and Away like a prizefighter answering the tenth round bell. Reaching back to extract the fold of bunny suit that had caught in the closing door, she announced, "I gotta have a cup of coffee."

Jan stood up in a haze of cigarette smoke to pour two cups. "Honey, we got a late call asking for you. Can you flog yourself to one more delivery?"

Groaning, Kate dropped into a straight chair, leaned to one side to rearrange the lump of tail, and thanked Jan for the coffee. After a cautious sip, she said, "Sure. It's only 8:15. Where to?"

"Well," Jan began reluctantly, rummaging on the desk for her order pad. "It's pretty far out. Maybe you should take Selma for backup, since it'll be late when you get there." Finding the request, she tilted it toward the light. "I told him we don't usually deliver to Golden, but he said he'd pay the mileage and you'd been there before."

Fatigue disappeared like magic. "Golden?"

"It's a commercial building, he said. Called CROPS."

"I know it," Kate rejoiced. "What am I supposed to take or sing or whatever?"

Jan read from the pad. "Wear harem outfit. Bring two dozen balloons just like the one you left last time. Dr. Garrett Brody's his name." Seeing Kate's expression, she added, "Oh, is that the guy you brought here one night? Ohh, uh-huh."

Leaping up, Kate danced toward the locker room. "Jan, you should definitely, absolutely, positively not wait up for me on this delivery."

THE MILD NIGHT BLEW THROUGH Kate's sunroof and loosened her perfect, upswept hairdo. Dark miles slipped under the tires as fast as the speed limit and winding road allowed. To Golden, through it, up the last stretch to the lab.

The music on the radio, drum-heavy and full of minor chords, matched her excited mood when she turned into the corrugated dirt lane. The Victorian outline loomed into view, no lights visible. What if Jan had got the date wrong? Maybe it's tomorrow. And how could Kate ever wait that long?

Jouncing around the driveway to the rear lot, she exhaled the breath she'd been holding. The back porch and kitchen lights shone expectantly. And as her headlights swept the building in a parking arc, the hallway lit up and Garrett's silhouette appeared at the back door.

Jumping out of the car, she strode across the dirt yard, oblivious to the dangers of potholes and rocks. "Evening, mister. You the one who ordered the pizza?"

"No, sorry. Wrong house," he said, swinging the door wide open to her.

"That's good because I didn't bring any. Woof!" This last was due to his hearty hug that literally took her breath away.

"Let's get all the serious stuff out of the way first," he said into her hair. "I'm sorry. You're sorry. Let's go make love. Did you bring the balloons?"

Laughing, she locked arms around his waist and tried to match his strength. "You don't get off that easy. You were going to prove to me you'd dropped your grudge."

"How about if I learned a magic trick, to show you I respect your profession?" His vicelike grip loosened to let her lean back and look at him.

"Great. Which trick would you like to learn? Please don't say you'll saw me in half."

"No, no. I've already learned one. It'll knock your socks off." He swung her sideways to eye her bare sandaled feet— "Too late, I see." His eyes raked upward past the gauze pantaloons to the harem bra. "Maybe it'll knock some other garment off instead."

Squirming out of the embrace, she stepped away, adjusted the jingling, fake gold necklace, and tried to look stern. "I'm a pretty tough audience."

"I know how to soften you up," he said, drawing her close again, sliding his gentle lips across hers with tantalizing slowness until he found the fit that settled into a cherishing kiss.

Kate felt tears behind her eyelids, longing for this moment to last, imagining that heaven must be Garrett holding her—and no interruptions. When his hand coasted down her bare midriff to knead her scantily clad bottom, she smiled. When his other hand prowled around to the front to insert a finger under the halter and trace the swell of one breast, she sighed and slumped into him.

"When the phone rings, don't answer," she murmured.

"The phone's going to ring?" he whispered against her cheek.

"If not the phone, something else. Someone will knock on the door. A plane will crash into the roof. Something."

"That's why I brought you all the way out here." He held her away from him to show her his wink. "I've got the perfect place for us."

"Not the cellar," she squeaked as he tucked her under one arm and steered them along the hall.

"You don't like your loving down and dirty?"

Giggling, she tried to elbow him in the ribs. There was a brief tickling match, and then they continued up the hall, his arm in a loose hammerlock around her neck. He stopped them by the unmarked door with the glass window.

"Sensory deprivation?" she asked, one eyebrow high. "Are you sure that's what you want?"

Swinging the door open, he gave her an impatient little push in the small of her back. She stopped just inside and took off her shoes on the plush carpet, reconsidering the room. Mellow pink lighting. No windows and one, lockable, door. No telephone. Soundproof walls. A reclining chair and an expanse of soft floor. Ideal.

She turned around and dragged him inside with her, snapping the door shut and yanking down the black blind on the little viewing window. The door lock depressed with a gratifying click.

"Now, my proud handsome," she gloated. "No one can hear your screams."

He reached for her and she twirled gracefully out of range. "Not so fast. First let's see the magic trick." She dropped cross-legged to the floor and looked attentive.

Scrubbing the back of his neck with the palm of his hand, Garrett stared at his feet. "Umm. It's kind of a combination magic trick and striptease."

"What?" She snickered. "Sounds wonderful. Please proceed."

"Uhh, I need a little audience participation, too." With one hand shading his eyes, he twisted in every direction, pretending to see her for the first time. "You. In the genie suit. Would you help me out here?"

"Genie suit!" She let him pull her up, let him hold her hand.

"Now then, I want you to pretend that you are mad about me, you can't keep your hands off me, you want to rip my clothes off and make passionate love to me. Think you can handle that?"

"Gee, I don't think I'm that good an actress," Kate sputtered through her laughter.

"Start with the shirt." He pointed to the buttons and let go of her hand so she could oblige.

"Are you sure there's a magic trick in this somewhere?" she said, enjoying the strip of male chest gradually coming into view. "Last button." She patted his flat stomach.

"Now pretend there's a drumroll while you take hold here and pull this shirttail out." To give the game more ambience, he muttered a quiet, "Boom-a-ta-rah-ta-ta—"

Grinning with expectation, Kate worked the shirt up and out and found the red silk scarf tied to the tail. Pulling steadily, bringing out the blue scarf attached to the red, she doubled over to laugh a moment before continuing to haul out the string of multicolored scarves.

"Six, seven," she counted out loud, still pulling. "How many could you get inside those tight jeans? Nine, and oh no!"

The tenth and last scarf had come free, dragging with it Garrett's baby blue bikini briefs. Kate collapsed on the floor with the colorful rope wadded in her lap, and laughed into her hands.

"You didn't read the secret message!" He stooped to search out the underwear again.

"Machine wash and tumble dry?" she guessed just before he spread them on her knee, the unevenly spaced, black block letters toward her.

Marry me, they said.

Swallowing hard, she lightly stroked each word with a suddenly trembling forefinger.

"I did it with Magic Marker," he said brightly.

"Oh, Garrett," she rejoiced, throwing arms around his neck, tipping them both full length onto the floor. "You'd better never make me sue for brief of promise. Breach. *Breach* of promise."

With Kate's soft curves crushed against him, Garrett found he was breathing as hard as if he'd run a mile. She loved him. She'd marry him. Relief and desire pumped through him; he could have lifted her over his head with one hand.

Instead, he slid fingers into her hair, destroying what was left of the topknot, and kissed her forehead. "I've missed you like hell." Fumbling behind her in search of a way to undo the frivolous bra, he repeated, "I've missed you."

"I'm glad." "Glad" was hardly the word to describe how she was feeling as he gave up and pulled the bra above her nipples.

"Your delicious sense of humor. I missed that almost as much as—" he paused to dip his face to the wealth he'd uncovered "—your delicious body."

She caught her breath, partly because of what he'd said, mostly because of what he was doing. "That's terrific," seemed to cover both. She let go of his hard shoulders to reach behind her back, undo the halter, and sail it across the room.

She started to do the same with the annoying necklace, but he stopped her. "It's sexy like that."

His warm, wet mouth wiped lazy circles on each breast, licked and nibbled at the swollen tips, made her eyes roll shut. He muttered intermittent words against her moistened skin: "I—want—to—love—you—beautiful—Kate—Kate—"

"Garrett," she sighed, sliding fingers into the front waistband of his jeans. The snap popped open, filling her with the thrill of anticipation. Scraping denim aside, she found and freed the silky hardness that would ease the gnawing emptiness she'd felt since the last time Garrett had loved her.

Moaning, she helped him strip the harem pants down and away. His broad hand went immediately to the place she wanted it most, touching lightly, teasing deeper, till the exploring became a wonderful, relentless stroke. Sucking air through clenched teeth, she fought off climax, tried to pull away from the certainty of it.

As if he'd read her mind, Garrett whispered, "Let go, Kate. There's more where this came from."

And so she did. Clutching his wide back, scrubbing full length against him, legs to legs, pelvis to pelvis, chest to chest, she vibrated with love. Only her face tilted away from him in a soundless cry of joy. Before she could stop shuddering, he was on top of her, in her, prolonging her release with his own exultant spasms.

Eventually the aftershocks dwindled, and both of them could move and talk again. They held each other and muttered foolish, meaningless things that neither of them could have repeated straight-faced, fully dressed, in bright daylight. Talk led to touch led to an encore, this time with Kate taking the lead. Her breasts swayed gently to the gliding to and fro that dampened Garrett's forehead with sweat till she climaxed and he did, too.

Panting, she fell forward and buried her nose in his neck. His circling hand on her back massaged her into a state of drowsiness. "Boy, am I glad I'm not home watching TV," she mumbled enigmatically.

"I'm glad you're not, too. Or doing anything else anywhere else." He thought a minute. "*With* anyone else."

"Wait till you hear how I turned down a trip to an exotic land because of you." She scooted loose and sat up to examine her knees. "I think I've got third-degree rug burns."

"What exotic land?"

"Actually, knowing Bing, probably Siberia."

Lying flat on his back, Garrett brushed some hair out of her eyes and waited till she looked into his. "I love you more than an hour ago. More than five minutes ago. As soon as the words are out, it's gone up another degree in intensity."

Kate stared gravely at the marvelous face under hers, not one trace of teasing in its expression. "I love you like that too, like a magic cup that's always full. It must be sleight of heart."

He took her hand to kiss the palm. Hitching up on his elbow, head on fist, he announced, "But whoa, let's not get too maudlin here. After this little recess is over, what do you say you stretch out in that chair wrong way up, feet on the headrest, and let me put Ping-Pong balls on your eyes, and see if you can guess which part of your anatomy I'm about to touch with which part of my anatomy?"

She narrowed her eyes, considering. "That plastic covering would probably stick to my skin and make disgusting noises when I wriggle."

"Hey, I hope so." His leer relaxed into a happy smile. "Did I mention I'd missed you? Yeah, I did. But the last straw was this evening when I stopped for gasoline at the self-serve."

"Gas reminds you of me?" She wrinkled her nose in dismay.

"Did you ever notice," he said, eyes crinkling with the coming wisecrack, "how erotic pumping gas is? When you slide that long nozzle into the gaping gas tank?"

She butted her head into his musky chest and sprawled in the strong welcome of his arms. "Fill 'er up."

Epilogue

October 29

Hi Captain,

First, thanks for the wedding gift of complimentary tickets to your Moscow performance. Garrett and I decided we couldn't justify the expense involved in taking advantage of them, but the thought did count.

You missed a great wedding. I wore a pink and orange chiffon toga, carried a birdcage full of purple orchids and white doves, and Garrett looked magnificent in a white, sequined tux with matching shoes. Since there was no male to give me away and no aisle to walk down—Mile High Stadium was closed, so we settled for their parking lot— I magically appeared beside the organist in a puff of smoke during the playing of "Come on, Baby, Light My Fire."

Does your ESP tell you that I'm lying through my lips, gums and teeth?

Actually we were married—a month ago already—in a lovely outdoor ceremony on the CROPS grounds, in a side yard with a mountain and meadow backdrop. There are just enough gold and white aspen up there to sparkle against the dark evergreens. Garrett, who turns out to be as romantic and almost as theatrical as I am, suggested I drive in an open carriage pulled by two sleek, ebony geldings, much the way a real Victorian bride might have done at this very same spot.

So I dressed the part—whispery blue sateen with a bustle, peach lace on the bell sleeves and a matching lace jabot. Headdress: a veiled, pastel blue Langtry bonnet. Footwear: black ribbed stockings and black, high-topped lace-ups. Jewelry: pearl stud earrings and a gold watch on a long neckchain. Underwear: but enough about me....

Garrett was gorgeous in a gray frock coat, striped trousers, gold silk vest, and a ruffled shirt so white it glowed. He looked as if he could deal you a straight flush easy as pie. All he lacked was the walrus mustache, which there hadn't been enough time to grow and he refused to stick on a fake one.

Since this was a costume wedding, attendants Minda and Selma came as Calamity Jane and Mother Hubbard respectively. The groomsmen were Mac Thayer—who wore buffalo hunter's garb—and Dog Smedley—who wore nothing. Because he ate his carnation necktie.)

There wasn't really an organist, just a tape deck playing New Age music, and Rudy Garcia actually gave me away. He says I'm the daughter he never had, thank goodness. (I'm sure you'll know how to read that, having probably felt the same way about me at times.) He wore a Billy the Kid duster, snowshoes, I kid you not, and used what looked like a cattle prod for his cane. Luckily, he didn't have to do any prodding. I didn't dawdle on the walk to the altar, just in case.

Using all the diplomacy I possess, I talked the aunts into letting someone else do the catering. It helped that their latest interest was photography, and they were willing to be the official candid camerawomen instead. If there is ever a contest involving the best videotape footage of sky and kneecaps, they're a shoo-in.

When we planned this wedding, we agreed it might be cool at the end of September, but if we kept the ceremony short and had plenty of booze to warm up the crowd, holding it outside would be okay. If it rained, we'd use the lab's front porch, which is big enough for thirty people if everyone stands straight with their arms down at their sides. But happy day, it didn't rain. It snowed. A lot.

The man with the horses substituted a sleigh for the carriage, I wore a navy cloak over my beautiful dress, pinned my white carnation nosegay to an imitation fur muff, and, as I've said, Mr. Garcia snowshoed me to the red rock altar. When we'd done our "I do's," Garrett and I kissed without even worrying about whether our mouths would stick fast—that might have been fun, actually.

Then the guests let go of their blue and white helium balloons. The sight of those bobbing, swooping messages of joy rising into the gray sky through the fat, white snowflakes was the most thrilling thing I've ever seen, even better than your tiki torch and silver sword routine.

We did have the reception inside. Garrett's sister Ann successfully bullied the caterers into adding hot chocolate to the menu at no extra charge. (Hey, it occurs to me you two have a lot in common. Wanna meet her?)

Joe, the custodian, had spit and polished the whole downstairs; you could have eaten off the floor, and Smedley did.

When we were able to take our leave without appearing impolite, Garrett and I slithered to his car while the well-wishers threw a little rice and a lot of snowballs. As we drove out of range, the party was deteriorating into a snowball free-for-all.

Moscow was a little too far, but we did make it to Las Vegas for a honeymoon, where I proved once and for all that any ESP I possess has nothing to do with roulette.

Now we're living in Garrett's apartment till we can find a nice, cheap, old painted lady, something on the order of the lab, to renovate and fill with little warlocks and witches.

Captain, I really do appreciate all you've done for me, including—and especially—sending me to Mister Smith-Garcia. Thanks for teaching me about magic. I can take it from here.

Love,
Kathy the Great

PASSPORT TO ROMANCE VACATION SWEEPSTAKES

OFFICIAL RULES

SWEEPSTAKES RULES AND REGULATIONS. NO PURCHASE NECESSARY.

HOW TO ENTER:

1. To enter, complete this official entry form and return with your invoice in the envelope provided, or print your name, address, telephone number and age on a plain piece of paper and mail to: Passport to Romance, P.O. Box #1397, Buffalo, N.Y. 14269-1397. No mechanically reproduced entries accepted.
2. All entries must be received by the Contest Closing Date, midnight, December 31, 1990 to be eligible.
3. Prizes: There will be ten (10) Grand Prizes awarded, each consisting of a choice of a trip for two people to: i) London, England (approximate retail value $5,050 U.S.); ii) England, Wales and Scotland (approximate retail value $6,400 U.S.); iii) Caribbean Cruise (approximate retail value $7,300 U.S.); iv) Hawaii (approximate retail value $ 9,550 U.S.); v) Greek Island Cruise in the Mediterranean (approximate retail value $12,250 U.S.); vi) France (approximate retail value $7,300 U.S.).
4. Any winner may choose to receive any trip or a cash alternative prize of $5,000.00 U.S. in lieu of the trip.
5. Odds of winning depend on number of entries received.
6. A random draw will be made by Nielsen Promotion Services, an independent judging organization on January 29, 1991, in Buffalo, N.Y, at 11:30 a.m. from all eligible entries received on or before the Contest Closing Date. Any Canadian entrants who are selected must correctly answer a time-limited, mathematical skill-testing question in order to win. Quebec residents may submit any litigation respecting the conduct and awarding of a prize in this contest to the Régie des loteries et courses du Quebec.
7. Full contest rules may be obtained by sending a stamped, self-addressed envelope to: "Passport to Romance Rules Request", P.O. Box 9998, Saint John, New Brunswick, E2L 4N4.
8. Payment of taxes other than air and hotel taxes is the sole responsibility of the winner.
9. Void where prohibited by law.

PASSPORT TO ROMANCE VACATION SWEEPSTAKES

OFFICIAL RULES

SWEEPSTAKES RULES AND REGULATIONS. NO PURCHASE NECESSARY.

HOW TO ENTER:

1. To enter, complete this official entry form and return with your invoice in the envelope provided, or print your name, address, telephone number and age on a plain piece of paper and mail to: Passport to Romance, P.O. Box #1397, Buffalo, N.Y. 14269-1397. No mechanically reproduced entries accepted.
2. All entries must be received by the Contest Closing Date, midnight, December 31, 1990 to be eligible.
3. Prizes: There will be ten (10) Grand Prizes awarded, each consisting of a choice of a trip for two people to: i) London, England (approximate retail value $5,050 U.S.); ii) England, Wales and Scotland (approximate retail value $6,400 U.S.); iii) Caribbean Cruise (approximate retail value $7,300 U.S.); iv) Hawaii (approximate retail value $ 9,550 U.S.); v) Greek Island Cruise in the Mediterranean (approximate retail value $12,250 U.S.); vi) France (approximate retail value $7,300 U.S.).
4. Any winner may choose to receive any trip or a cash alternative prize of $5,000.00 U.S. in lieu of the trip.
5. Odds of winning depend on number of entries received.
6. A random draw will be made by Nielsen Promotion Services, an independent judging organization on January 29, 1991, in Buffalo, N.Y., at 11:30 a.m. from all eligible entries received on or before the Contest Closing Date. Any Canadian entrants who are selected must correctly answer a time-limited, mathematical skill-testing question in order to win. Quebec residents may submit any litigation respecting the conduct and awarding of a prize in this contest to the Régie des loteries et courses du Quebec.
7. Full contest rules may be obtained by sending a stamped, self-addressed envelope to: "Passport to Romance Rules Request", P.O. Box 9998, Saint John, New Brunswick, E2L 4N4.
8. Payment of taxes other than air and hotel taxes is the sole responsibility of the winner.
9. Void where prohibited by law.

 RLS-DIR

PASSPORT TO ROMANCE
WIN 1 of 10 Vacations SEE INSIDE

VACATION SWEEPSTAKES

MONTH 3 ENTRY

Official Entry Form

Yes, enter me in the drawing for one of ten Vacations-for-Two! If I'm a winner, I'll get my choice of any of the six different destinations being offered — and I won't have to decide until after I'm notified!

Return entries with invoice in envelope provided along with Daily Travel Allowance Voucher. Each book in your shipment has two entry forms — and the more you enter, the better your chance of winning!

Name ______________________________

Address ______________________________ Apt.

City ______________ State/Prov. ______________ Zip/Postal Code

Daytime phone number ______________________________
Area Code

☐ I am enclosing a Daily Travel Allowance Voucher in the amount of $__________ Write in amount revealed beneath scratch-off

PASSPORT TO ROMANCE
WIN 1 of 10 Vacations SEE INSIDE

VACATION SWEEPSTAKES

MONTH 3 ENTRY

Official Entry Form

Yes, enter me in the drawing for one of ten Vacations-for-Two! If I'm a winner, I'll get my choice of any of the six different destinations being offered — and I won't have to decide until after I'm notified!

Return entries with invoice in envelope provided along with Daily Travel Allowance Voucher. Each book in your shipment has two entry forms — and the more you enter, the better your chance of winning!

Name ______________________________

Address ______________________________ Apt.

City ______________ State/Prov. ______________ Zip/Postal Code

Daytime phone number ______________________________
Area Code

☐ I am enclosing a Daily Travel Allowance Voucher in the amount of $__________ Write in amount revealed beneath scratch-off

CPS-THREE